A LOVE STORY STRAIGHT OUT OF SAINT LOUIS

THE FINALE

A Novel by
Summer Johnson-Booker

To submit a manuscript for our review,

email us at

submissions@majorkeypublishing.com

<u>Acknowledgements</u>

I want to thank my family and friends, who have been supportive of me in my journey as a new author. The experience has been amazing, and I appreciate you all.

CHAPTER ONE

"How you feeling, fam?" Kerry asked his brother. He noticed that he had been moving around a lot better.

"I'm good. Can't complain."

"I haven't seen Stacey around here lately. You decided to cut her loose?"

"Naw, man, I kinda fucked up." Corey rubbed his head, thinking back on the last conversation that he and Stacey had.

"What you mean you fucked up?" Kerry continued to pry. He knew that Corey didn't like owning up to his mistakes, but he wanted to know what happened between him and Stacey. He was the one that brought her to the house in the first place.

"Man, listen, when you first brought Stacey over here, there was an instant connection for me. I mean, she was fine as hell, but she was all about her business. For a long time, she wouldn't give me no play, but as time went on and with my persistence, she gave in and she started falling for me. It didn't take long before things got physical. We were intimate pretty much every day, and then it got to the point where that's all we would do when she came over. I was already healing and able to take care of myself. I actually started catching feelings for her."

"So you had me continuing to pay her, and all y'all were doing was fucking? I was paying for you to have sex?" Kerry reiterated.

"If you wanted to have sex, I could have gotten you a prostitute. That's all she turned out to be anyway."

Corey laughed. "It wasn't planned that way; it just happened."

"Anyway, I started feeling a tight bond with her. I thought she was someone that I could trust and be one hundred with, so I asked her to do something for me."

At that point, Kerry was very interested in the conversation. He knew that his brother was not that easy to get along with, so for Stacey to fall for him so fast, he must have really been putting it on her, or maybe his conversation was just that good.

"Okay, quit stalling, bro. What did you ask her?" Kerry rushed, leaning forward to make sure that he didn't miss anything.

"I came up with a plan, and I asked her to go to the hospital that Jasmine was going to deliver the baby at and kidnap my baby once it was born."

Kerry's eyes grew large after hearing his brother's confession. He often wondered how, as identical twins, they could be so different. Kerry knew that he wasn't perfect, but he felt like his twin brother was crazy in every sense of the word.

"Nigga, you did what?" Kerry blurted out.

"Man, look, I know that it ain't right, but I know that she's not going to let me see my child either."

"And when she finds out that it was you that put Stacey up to this, she really ain't gone let you see the baby. You fucked up big time, bruh. I can't get you out of this one. I wouldn't even know where to start," Kerry told him.

"But ain't you your brother's keeper?" Corey asked his brother before he walked out of the room.

"I'm your brother, and I'm your keeper, but I'm not your fool, Corey. You can't put me up under this much pressure, bro. This ain't like the petty shit you usually get into. Nigga, this is serious. I can't keep getting wrapped up in your foolishness. This shit has gotten way out of hand. Besides, what can I do? If that girl finds out that you are behind this and she gets the law involved, it will be nothing I can do anyway."

Kerry walked out of the room and into the bathroom.

Corey sat there with his hands covering his face. He knew that he was in a fucked-up situation, and he knew that he had put Stacey in a fucked-up situation as well. He felt bad for it too because he did actually like her. He liked her just like he liked Jasmine when they first started talking. He was hoping that Stacey would be able to prove her loyalty to him early in the relationship, and she didn't. He gave her an important task, and she dropped the ball, but she was a good girl. He knew that he should have known better than to involve her in something like that.

"Where is the baby now? Is it with Stacey?" Kerry asked when he walked back into the room with Corey.

"Naw, she couldn't go through with the plan, so the baby is still at the hospital. She got nervous after taking the baby and left him in the bathroom on the floor."

"Aww man!" Kerry exclaimed as he paced back and forth on the hardwood floor.

"You know this is some bullshit, right?"

"Man, how many times are you going to tell me this? You can't make me feel any worse than I already do," Corey told him.

"I'm not trying to make you feel bad. I'm sure you already feel like shit. I just want you to start thinking before you go including people in your shit, man. Stacey got a kid at home. You don't know what I had to do to get her to come here and help you in the first place. Hell, the lil' money I was paying her to help you get well wasn't worth the shit you were putting her through. And you talking about a brother's keeper, but nigga, we got the same damn face. Have you ever heard of mistaken identity?" Kerry stood there looking at his brother waiting for him to say something, but he never did. Corey knew that it wasn't anything that he could say.

"I got to go," Kerry said as he turned his back on his brother to walk away.

"You just gon' leave, man? You're not going to tell me

what to do?" Corey asked his brother following him to the front door.

"What do you want me to say? I don't know what to tell you. I can't give you the answers for this one bro," Kerry told him before leaving.

Corey didn't know what to do next. He picked up the phone to call Stacey. He felt bad for snapping on her the last time he talked to her. He dialed her number, but instead of pushing the call button, he canceled it. He knew that she wouldn't want to talk to him. He sat quietly for a minute to be one with his thoughts, but his thoughts were killing him.

He picked up the phone again and dialed Stacey's number. This time, he let the call connect, but he didn't get an answer. After four rings, his call went to voicemail, and he decided not to leave her a message.

Corey got up off the couch and headed to the kitchen. He was originally going to get a beer out of the refrigerator, but when he saw a bottle of Hennessy on the counter, he opened the bottle and drank that instead. He was at such a loss. He knew that people thought he was crazy because he never hesitated to pop off on somebody if he felt the need to, but he really wasn't as crazy as he seemed. He just didn't think things through before he did them most of the time. He always felt justified while he was doing all these outrageous things, but once everything calmed down and the adrenaline rush was over, he realized how wrong he really was.

CHAPTER TWO

Jasmine stayed her mandatory four days in the hospital following her cesarean section. The hospital staff had been watching over baby Malcolm like a hawk. Everybody made sure that they knew where he was at all times. Although Jasmine appreciated the extra attention her baby was getting, it was hard for her to sleep after his abduction because she was up constantly watching over him too. She allowed Anthony to leave so that he could get some fresh air as long as he didn't leave her for too long. That was the only way she could get some rest. To know that Anthony was there, awake, and alert to watch her son.

Continuous room service was great, and the nurses were nice, but Jasmine wanted nothing more than to be in her home with her son and her man. She was ready for the drama to be over, so they could start the rest of their lives together. Her nurse had already told her that she would be discharged soon, and that they would be able to leave.

She walked around her hospital room to make sure that she wasn't leaving anything behind as she packed up her and Malcolm's belongings. It was painful for her to be up moving around so soon after her C-section, but she couldn't let that slow down her process of getting out of there as soon as possible.

She knew that if she asked Anthony to pack their bags that he would leave things behind, and besides that, she was tired of asking him to do basic things for her anyway. He had helped her wash up in the shower, wipe herself after using the bathroom, walk from here to there, and sit up to eat. She knew that having a C-Section would hurt from all of the books she read, but she didn't imagine the recovery part of it being so bad too. As long as she had medicine in her, she could manage to do a little more, but once the medicine wore off, she was back to being helpless.

"Hey, babe, have they discharged you yet?" Anthony asked, sounding winded.

"Not yet," Jasmine replied.

"Why are you breathing like that?" she asked him.

"I rushed back up here so that I could help you. I knew that your hard-headed ass would be up doing the stuff that me and the nurse told you not to do. I don't want you to hurt yourself. You need to heal."

"Anthony, quit trippin' I'm good."

Here he goes with this overprotective shit again. I can't wait to be back at one hundred percent, Jasmine thought to herself.

"Jas, baby, I'm just here to help. With whatever you need me to do," Anthony told her feeling like a nuisance to her. That's the last thing that he wanted to be, but he didn't know how else to show his love and support for her. He didn't want her to feel like she had to be strong and do things that she really couldn't do only to be right back in the hospital because she wouldn't allow herself to heal.

"Well, the car is pulled around the front whenever you are ready to go," Anthony told her before walking out of the room.

At that moment, Jasmine felt a little bad because she knew that she was probably making him feel like he was a bother, but he was, and even though she didn't want to just come out and say, "you are getting on my nerves," her attitude let him know without her saying the words.

Anthony took a walk down to the nursery just to peek in at baby Malcolm. He stayed in the hallway and just looked through the window.

"Hey, how are you? Are you guys ready for me to bring him down to your room?" one of the nursery workers asked. After seeing Anthony standing in the hallway.

"No. I'm just looking at him. His mom will call down here when she's ready for him."

"Oh okay. No problem," the nurse said, looking perplexed before going back inside the nursery.

Anthony stood right in the window. He quietly counted Malcolm's ten fingers and ten toes. He was one of the only babies in the room that wasn't crying or fussing. He was pretty content. He thought about the responsibility of caring for a child. Out of all the women he'd been with, he had never had any children of his own, but as soon as he found the one woman he'd always been in love with, she was pregnant with someone else's child.

What am I getting myself into? he wondered.

After spending so much time with Jasmine, it was no doubt in his mind, body, or spirit that he still loved her. He had nurtured her through a whole pregnancy in which he had nothing to do with. He had seen sides of her that he didn't know existed. He finally got the opportunity to make love to her. Not quite the way he'd imagined it being the first time, but it was still beautiful to him. He met her closest friends and some family, and they all seemed nice and welcomed him with open arms, and not to mention, the Corey drama.

"Mr. Williams, I'm going to take the baby down to his mother now so that you can get him ready for his ride home. Do you have his car seat ready?" the nurse asked, peeking out of the door of the nursery.

"Oh, I left it in the car. I'll go get it and meet you in the room."

He hurried outside to his car, retrieved the baby's car seat, and headed upstairs. He took his time this time around. He didn't want to rush. He wanted to give Jasmine all the time that she needed to get herself together. He figured that if she needed anything, there were enough nurses there to help her.

Arriving back to the room, baby Malcolm was already

bundled up and ready to go. Jasmine had all her things packed up on a cart, and all that was left was to put the baby in his seat. Jasmine handed her son over to Anthony, and he did his best to strap him into his car seat.

"What's so funny?" Anthony asked when he heard Jasmine giggling from across the room.

"You did it wrong," she told him, still giggling.

Anthony stepped back to take a look at his handy work.

"Looks good to me," he protested.

"Let me show you how it's done," the discharge nurse told him.

He stood close by and watched the nurse correctly strap the baby in his car seat.

"Voila," she said when she was done.

"I almost had it," Anthony told them.

Jasmine and the nurse laughed at Anthony. He didn't mind; he laughed too.

"Alright, let's go," Jasmine said. She was more than ready to get out of there.

"I was in the hospital a few months ago after getting shot and this time to have a baby. I wouldn't care if I never saw the inside of a hospital again. I'm just ready to go home," Jasmine proclaimed.

Anthony wheeled Jasmine and Malcolm down to the nurse's station as the nurse pushed the cart full of their belongings. The nurse at the desk cut the hospital bracelets off of Jasmine and Malcolm and sent them on their way.

Once sitting comfortably in the backseat of the car beside her son, Jasmine was able to finally take in a breath of fresh air. She was so happy to finally be headed home with her two men to start a new chapter in her life as a mommy and eventually, a wife. She often reflected on the day of her baby shower because that was the day that Anthony proposed to her.

She couldn't wait. Her friends had been helping her with the planning, and although they had a lot done already, there was still much more to be completed. She had even changed the design of her dress three times.

Jas snapped out of her thoughts about her wedding when she noticed that Anthony pulled the car up in front of her apartment building. She immediately tried to get out of the car but was stopped when she felt the strain of her incision.

"Aw shit!" she yelled out in pain.

"Damn, Jay, what are you doing? I was coming to help you," Anthony said as he ran around to her side of the car to assist her.

Jasmine burst out crying, which threw Anthony for a loop.

"What are you crying for, Jay, the stitches?" he asked.

"No," she managed to say in between sobs.

"Well, what is it?"

"I don't know. Just get Malcolm into the house, and then come back and get me," she told him not wanting him to know that him fussing at her kind of hurt her feelings. She just forgot for a split second that she couldn't move as good as she could before, but she wasn't going to tell him that. She figured that she was still hormonal from the effects of her pregnancy, crying because he raised his voice a little bit.

Without another word, Anthony did what he was told. He entered the apartment and sat the baby down on the living room floor while still in his car seat. When he went back outside to get Jasmine her face had cleared up, and it didn't look like she had ever been crying. He opened the door for her and held his arm out for her to hold on to. They took their time making their way up the stairs and into the apartment.

Jasmine sat on her couch and just watched her baby sleeping peacefully in his car seat. She was so in love already. She couldn't believe that God had chosen her of all people to be the one to grow that little boy in her womb and allowed her to be his mommy. She was so honored. She just hated that Corey had to be his biological father.

"Are you hungry?" Anthony asked her when he came back in the house from bringing in the rest of their things from the car.

"Not yet, but I will start pumping in a minute," she told him while rubbing her breasts. They had been so sore since her milk started coming in over the last day or so.

"Remember, there are not a lot of things that you can do on your own, so let me know when you want to do something."

"Okay."

Jasmine looked down at her phone when she felt it vibrate. Candice's name lit up on the screen.

"Hey," Jasmine answered.

"Hey, girl. How are you?" Candice asked.

"I'm fine, girl. We just got in the house from the hospital."

"Aw okay. Well, I won't bother you. You guys didn't have any more problems up there at the hospital, did you?" Candice asked, talking about the baby's almost abduction.

"No. Everything was good. We kept close tabs on Malcolm and with whatever was going on with him. They made sure someone knew where he was at all times. I'm just happy to be back at home. Now, I can monitor who is coming in and out, and I don't have to be bothered with anyone if I don't want to."

"I feel you on that. Well, am I somebody that you would want to be bothered with? I would like to see my godson," Candice said with a smile on her face. She knew that Jasmine wasn't going to deny her a visit.

"Come on, girl. How long will it be before you get here?"

"I can be there in about thirty minutes. I have to make one stop before I come."

"See you when you get here." Jasmine pushed the button on her phone to end the call.

Malcolm started to coo, and immediately, Jasmine jumped to see what was wrong with him.

"Baby, can you please bring Malcolm to me?" Jasmine shouted.

Anthony came into the living room and sat the car seat down on the couch next to Jasmine. She leaned over and unbuckled the straps and gently lifted the baby out of his seat.

"Oh come to Mommy, sweet baby," she said in her baby voice.

"Don't start that baby talk with him now. He'll be talking like that forever," Anthony told her while passing through the living room and going into the bathroom.

"That's fine with me. Mommy's little man can talk however he wants."

"Yeah okay. You women always think that stuff is cute until the baby is a grown ass man still talking and acting like a baby," Anthony commented with a snicker.

"He'll be fine as long as he has you to teach him differently," Jasmine told him, stroking his ego a little bit.

"You got that right. I'm going to make sure he's together 'cause you women ain't gon' do nothing but spoil him."

CHAPTER THREE

Candice came through Jasmine's front door like she lived there. She didn't even bother to knock. When Anthony heard the front door open, he immediately pulled his strap from his waistband.

"Girl, you can't just be walking up in people's house like that," Anthony said when he saw that it was Candice.

"Hands up! Don't shoot," Candice said when she saw the gun pointed at her.

Normally, Anthony wouldn't have been so quick to shoot somebody, but with all of the bullshit that they have been dealing with and with Corey on the loose, he had to be cautious.

Jasmine laughed at them both.

"Girl, yo' man was about to shoot me," Candice joked.

Anthony just went into the bedroom to continue doing what he was doing when Candice walked in. He didn't find the humor in it, but he knew that Candice was just clowning around, so he didn't put too much thought into it. Truth was, ever since Malcolm was taken from them at the hospital, he had been under so much pressure to keep them safe. He couldn't let anything like that happen again.

"Let me see TT's baby," Candice said as she reached over to take the baby from Jasmine.

"Oh wait. I have to go wash my hands first."

Candice went to the bathroom to wash her hands and came back to get the baby. She grabbed a receiving blanket and draped it over her shoulder and over her chest to protect the baby's skin from any germs or detergent on her shirt. She cradled the baby in her left arm and gently rocked him. Candice was in awe of how handsome he was. At that moment, she knew that he was going to be the most spoiled baby that ever came into her life because she was going to buy him everything she saw.

"Why is he so uptight?" she whispered to Jasmine about Anthony.

"He has become extra overprotective of us ever since the hospital incident."

"Well, I can understand that."

Candice continued to play with baby Malcolm. She enjoyed every moment of her time that she was able to spend with him his first time home. She sang to him, rocked him, and even helped Jasmine when it was time to try to breastfeed him.

While Jasmine sat there on the couch cradling her baby and nursing him, Candice watched on in amazement. She couldn't believe that after all that happened in their lives, she was there witnessing such a beautiful sight. Her best friend, was finally happy, in a relationship with a man that loved her unconditionally, and with a child of her own to love on so that she could heal from all of the bullshit she'd been through.

"You look pretty comfy over there. I guess I'll go and let you guys settle in. Is there anything you want or need for me to do for you before I leave?" Candice offered.

"You don't have to leave," Jasmine protested.

"I can come back whenever you need me to. I'm only a phone call away. If Anthony leaves, call me, and I'll come back to help. I'll even bring Jenna and Tamika with me."

"Fine, I don't need anything right now. Anthony will help me if I need anything right away."

"Okay then," Candice told her with a smile. She stood up and kissed Jasmine and Malcolm before grabbing her purse.

"Bye, Anthony!" she yelled down the hall so that Anthony would hear her.

"See ya!" he yelled back, standing in the doorway of the bedroom. He didn't bother coming all the way out of the room.

Candice waved at her friend, turned the lock on the doorknob to lock the door, and left.

"Come on, baby. Let's get you and Malcolm settled in the back," Anthony told Jasmine when he saw her dozing off on the couch.

Jasmine held on to baby Malcolm as Anthony held on to her. He led them down the hall and into the bedroom. Once she was comfortable, he went to get into the shower.

Anthony was so tired after the day he'd had from the excitement of finally being able to bring the baby home and finishing getting things taken care of around the house to make sure that Jasmine could move around without interfering with her incision.

After about fifteen minutes in the shower, he stepped out and dried off just to find Jasmine asleep in their bed, and the baby was swaddled and snuggled up in the co-sleeper attached to Jasmine's side of the bed.

Anthony smiled at the sight of them resting peacefully and laid down beside her. He flipped through the channels on the TV to find something to help him fall asleep.

"Oh, this my shit right here," he said when he saw *Harlem Nights* appear on the screen. Eddie Murphy was one of his favorite actors and comedians of all time.

It didn't take Anthony long to fall asleep at all. After a few laughs, he was out. The day had him exhausted, and he couldn't fight his sleep anymore.

Neither of them had been sleeping long before Jasmine heard her baby crying. She automatically thought that it was feeding time, so she started getting up and wiping the sleep out of her eyes.

When she looked over to where she laid her son down just a few hours ago, he wasn't there anymore. She thought that she was dreaming because she kept hearing him cry.

Jasmine sat straight up, not wanting to panic and

looked around her dark bedroom. She really did think that she was in a dream but couldn't be sure.

When she heard Malcolm's cries get louder and louder, it snapped her out of her trance and directed her attention toward her bedroom door.

She slid off the side of her bed and felt a tug at the bottom of her stomach. She was so determined to find her son that she forgot that she had stitches. She immediately put her hand on the incision as she grimaced in pain.

The pain and agony that she felt from her wound didn't stop her from moving along. Jasmine crept slowly to her bedroom door and down the hallway following the sound of her baby. She looked down at her hand that was holding her stomach and noticed blood on it.

Oh my God, I'm bleeding, she thought to herself.

She continued down her dark hallway, leaning against the wall for support. She walked past the bathroom door and past her linen closet. It seemed like the longest walk of her life. The closer she got, it appeared that her front door was cracked open a little bit.

What the hell is going on? I know Anthony never

forgets to lock the house down before he goes to bed, she thought.

She started moving a little quicker. When she made it to her living room, she saw her baby. He was still crying, and he was in the arms of his father.

Corey sat there on her couch with a grin on his face. It was not a happy grin but a sinister one. She knew that he came with nothing but evil intentions.

"Well, it took yo' ass long enough," he told her.

"Corey, give me my baby," she said as firmly as she could.

She didn't want to cry although she was in physical pain, and she was dying on the inside not knowing if Corey had hurt her son or not. At that point, he was still crying.

"Don't you mean *our* son?" he questioned.

"I don't want you to have anything to do with him, Corey. Give me my son," she said again, talking louder, but that didn't matter. Corey didn't budge.

"I sent a little girl to do a grown man's job, and she failed. She flaked on me, but I want my son, and I came here to get him."

"Corey, I am begging you. Please, give me Malcolm and leave," she pleaded, but it fell on deaf ears.

"Oh, that's what you named him? I was hoping that he'd be a junior."

At that moment, Jasmine wished that she was not in so much pain. She knew that if she didn't have her incision that she would have been able to get to Corey and her son. She wanted to kill Corey for what he was doing to her. She couldn't believe that he had the nerve to come into her house while she was sleeping and do something to this extreme. She didn't know what his motives were with her son, and she didn't want to find out either.

"Anthony!" she yelled out.

"Oh yeah, you wanna call captain save a hoe to come and save yo' ass? That lil' bitch can't touch me. He hasn't been able to get at me yet."

"Anthony!" Jasmine called out again, hoping that this time he would wake up and come save her child.

Corey stood up and looked at Jasmine. "You have always been a sorry piece of shit. I knew you would try to keep our child away from me. If I have it my way, Jasmine,

33

you will never see him again," he told her and headed for her front door still with baby Malcolm in his arms.

"Corey, please don't take him," she begged him, now with tears running down her face.

He didn't care about her begging and pleading. He didn't care about her crying or hurting her. That's what he wanted to do. He wanted to hurt her because she wanted to do all that she could to keep his child away from him. In his mind, she couldn't do that. She couldn't take his only son away from him. He thought that his son needed to be with his father, not with some man pretending to be.

Corey walked out of the front door of Jasmine's apartment carrying her son. Her whole body shook, and her knees buckled. She dropped to the floor in pain for herself and for her son. She heard her son cry out of the front door and down the steps.

She crawled to the door just in time to see Corey get into a car before it sped away. The car was already sitting out in front of her building. She couldn't see who was driving the car, but she was able to tell that it wasn't Corey's car. It was Anthony's car. The car that was stolen the night he and DeAndre were in the warehouse that they left Corey in. She couldn't believe that he was bold enough to drive that car to her house.

Jasmine didn't even bother closing her door. She used a table that was in her living room to pull herself up and tiptoed back toward her room.

Before she could get all the way down the hall, Anthony came walking out of the room rubbing his eyes.

"Hey, baby, is Malcolm okay?" he asked, thinking that she had gotten out of bed to feed him.

She didn't answer him. She kept crying.

"What's going on. Why is the door wide open?" he asked.

"Why didn't you wake me up to help you, Jas? You know you shouldn't be moving around a lot by yourself." Anthony was still oblivious to the situation. The light was off in the hallway, and he couldn't tell that Jasmine was in so much pain. All he knew was that he was asking questions, and she wouldn't answer him. He held her arm and helped her back to the bedroom. Then, he went and closed and locked the front door.

When he got back to the bedroom, he noticed that she had blood oozing from her stomach, and she was still crying. He turned on the light in the bedroom to get a better look at her and noticed that she looked like shit.

"Jasmine, baby, what's wrong? Where's Malcolm?" he asked, very concerned.

"Corey has Malcolm," she managed to say in between sobs.

That statement made Anthony's heart drop down to his feet.

"What do you mean he has him? How did he get him?"

"He came in here and took him. I heard him crying, and when I went to see what was wrong with him, I saw Corey holding him in the living room. Then, he left. He took my baby and drove off in your car."

Anthony didn't ask any more questions. He went to the closet and grabbed his black sweatpants and his matching black hoodie. He quickly got dressed. He grabbed a gun out of the back of the closet. He grabbed his keys, cell phone, a box of bullets, and left the apartment. He didn't say anything else to Jasmine. He just left her sitting in the chair in her bedroom.

Jasmine continued to cry. She knew what Anthony was going to do, and she just wanted him to return safely with her son. She called Candice to come over because she couldn't sit there alone. She knew that she would go crazy.

CHAPTER FOUR

It didn't take long for Candice to get to Jasmine's apartment. When she got there, she didn't bother to knock on the door. She just walked right in and straight to the bedroom where she heard Jasmine crying. She immediately got down on her knees in front of her friend and wrapped her arms around her waist, allowing Jasmine to rest her head on her shoulder.

"Jasmine, I know it seems impossible, baby, but I want you to try not to worry. You know that Anthony has everything under control. You have to have faith and believe that everything is going to work out." Candice did her best to console her friend, but she knew that it wasn't anything she could do or say to make her feel better about what happened.

"Candice, I felt so helpless. I couldn't do anything to protect my child. I just stayed there in one spot and watched that crazy ass lunatic carry my son out of this apartment. That's bullshit, Candice. He knew that with me just getting out of the hospital and me being hurt that I wouldn't be able to get to him. He's a coward for coming at me now." Jasmine stood up and attempted to pace her bedroom floor but was quickly reminded that she couldn't when she doubled over in pain.

"Let me get you cleaned up and back in the bed," Candice told her. She went to the hall closet and grabbed some clean towels to spread over the bed. Candice held her arm out so that Jasmine could hold on to her and lift herself up. She guided her to her bed and helped her get in it. Jasmine laid there thinking about her baby. She didn't care about anything else that was going on. She didn't care about being clean or anything, but she knew that Candice would fight her on it, so she just went with it. Candice had left the room and came back with a plastic tub of warm water, a clean washcloth, and a fresh pad. Exposing her incision from her cesarean section, she removed the old pad that was bloody and set it to the side. Using the washcloth and warm water, she gently dabbed the wound until it was clean. She folded a clean pad and placed it right on the incision and taped it in place. When she was done, she pulled the comforter over her legs and fluffed her pillows.

"When is the next time you are supposed to take your medicine?" Candice asked.

"I haven't taken it in a while, so I can take some now."

Candice grabbed the bottle of pain pills that sat on the nightstand next to the bed and handed two of them to Jasmine. She went to the kitchen to get her a glass of water to drink with her medicine.

Before going back into the bedroom, she stood in the hallway at the door and said a silent prayer for her friend. She didn't understand why Jasmine was being put through all that she was. She was a good person that cared for everybody. She just fucked up by getting involved with the wrong person. Corey had managed to turn her life upside down in just a few years.

Candice walked into the room and handed Jasmine her glass of water. She hoped that it was something in the medicine to make her drowsy so that she could fall asleep until they were able to hear something from Anthony. She figured that Jasmine sleeping would be the only way to keep her from stressing so much about her situation.

"I don't know what I'm going to do if Corey hurts my baby," Jasmine spoke after several minutes of silence. She was in a daze.

"He'll be fine, Jas. I know Anthony is going to take care of everything," Candice spoke the words, but she didn't sound too convinced herself of what she was saying.

Candice and Jasmine sat in silence. It was so much tension in the room, and Candice didn't know how to ease it. She didn't know what it was going to take to make her friend feel better other than her son being back at home with her.

Jasmine sat on her bed in a trance until she finally dozed off.

Candice was happy when she realized that Jasmine had finally fallen asleep.

She was feeling a bit uneasy, but she knew that her main reason for being there was to comfort her friend. She couldn't sit still too long, so she got up and started pacing the bedroom floor. She also walked the hall and kept peeking out of the living room window.

"About time," she said when she heard the St.

Lunatics's song "Breathe In Breathe Out" come out of her phone's speaker, indicating an incoming phone call.

"Girl, I got your text. What happened?" Tamika asked when Candice answered the phone.

"Jasmine is over here torn up because Corey came in her apartment and took Malcolm while she and Anthony were asleep."

"How the hell did he do that?" Tamika asked.

"Hell, I don't know, but she needs us. She needs our support!" Candice fussed.

"I'll be there when I can. Just keep me posted," Tamika replied nonchalantly.

Candice looked at her cell phone and pushed the button to end the call. At that very moment, she hated the fact that she wasn't on an old-school landline phone to slam it down into its cradle as hard as she could so that Tamika could really feel the frustration that she felt with her.

She immediately dialed Jenna's number. She was sure that Jasmine would not want everyone involved in her business, but she didn't care. They were going to find out anyway. Jasmine was hurting, and she couldn't hold her up alone. She needed the help of her sisters to help her carry the extra emotional weight.

She listened to the phone ring as she peeked out of the living room window. It was so dark. It seemed like the street lights that usually lit up the block at night were dim. The wind was blowing, and leaves were blowing around freely. It just didn't feel right to her.

"Hey, girl, are you busy?" Candice asked when Jenna sleepily answered the phone.

"I was sitting here watching a movie. What's up?"

"I need you to come sit with me and Jasmine. I already called Tamika, and I don't know if she's coming. She's on some bullshit as usual."

"What's going on though, why do you need me to sit with y'all?" Jenna asked, genuinely concerned.

"That punk ass nigga Corey came into Jasmine's apartment and took Malcolm while she and Anthony were sleeping, and she's fucked up."

"Shit, I would be too. I'll be there in a minute. Let me throw some clothes on."

Jenna got up off of her couch and went to get dressed.

She thought that she would be able to stay in for the night for the first time in weeks. She had been working double shifts at her job just so that she could pay for all the things that she needed for Jasmine's wedding, and now, she didn't even know if there was going to be a wedding.

"I'm so damn sick of this motherfucker. I could kill him myself," Jenna mumbled to herself as she slid her jacket on over her Polo T-Shirt. She grabbed the rest of her things and headed straight to Jasmine's house.

When Jasmine finally woke up, Jenna and Candice were sitting at her bedside. She remembered telling Candice not to call anyone else, but hell, Jenna was already there now. She'd better make the best of it.

"Where's Tamika?" Jasmine asked, trying to sound welcoming of her friends being there.

"I talked to her. She said that she'd be here," Candice said just before the doorbell rang.

Candice jumped up to see who it was at the door.

"Speaking of the devil," she said when she opened the door to let Tamika in.

"Jasmine was just asking about you," Candice told her

"What's up, y'all?" Tamika asked.

"Hey," Jenna replied.

"How are you doing, Jas?" Tamika asked, sounding concerned.

"I want my son back home with me where it's safe."

Jasmine felt like there was something different with Tamika, but she couldn't put her finger on exactly what it was, so she just shook it off.

"Has anyone heard anything from Anthony yet?" Jasmine asked.

"No," everyone answered in unison.

Jasmine just burst out into tears. She couldn't believe what was happening to her. It seemed as though the drama never stopped.

"Is there anything you need us to do for you right now?" Jenna asked as she stroked Jasmine's hair.

"I only want my baby. If you guys can't go get him and bring him back home, then it's nothing you can do for me."

"Hmph." Tamika huffed and rolled her eyes.

"Tamika, what is your problem? Why are you even here? It always seems like you have an issue with me, and

I don't understand why because I ain't never did anything to you!" Jasmine yelled.

Tamika didn't respond. She didn't answer any of Jasmine's questions. She sat on a chair that was across from the bed and just stared at Jasmine, which pissed Jasmine off even more.

"The questions weren't rhetorical. I need answers. What is your problem? See, I wish I didn't have these damn stitches because I would walk over there and slap the shit out of you. What are you rolling your eyes for?" Jasmine was hot. She was about to go from zero to one hundred real quick, or at least, she wanted to. Those stitches were the only thing holding her back from getting to Tamika, and Jasmine didn't usually flip like that, but she was sick of Tamika. She felt like every time she came around, she had an attitude about something.

"Jasmine, chill, man. It ain't worth it," Jenna tried to talk some sense into her.

"Man, fuck that shit!" Jasmine yelled.

"You know what, I do have a problem. I'm tired of always being caught up in your drama. It's always something with you, Jasmine. It's like the bullshit always follows you, and you always bring everybody into it. We are always here for you, to comfort you, to make sure you are okay, and to pick up the pieces to your fucked up puzzle." Tamika stood up and finally spoke her mind.

"That's how you really fell, huh?" Jasmine asked already knowing that it was. "That's fucked up, Tamika. We've been girls for how long, and you feeling like this about me? You act like I asked for any of this stuff to happen to me. You act like I wanted these things to occur. This is the type of shit that happens when you dealing with a crazy person like Corey. Nobody in their right mind would want this kind of shit to happen to anybody, and if it were happening to you, I'd be there without a doubt. That's what friends are for... at least that's what I thought." Jasmine tried to be tough, but she couldn't keep the tears from flowing. She was hurt about the situation with her son being gone and about what Tamika said to her. She and Tamika had been friends for years and had never had a real beef until then.

"Tamika, you know you are dead ass wrong right

now," Candice told her.

"That's another thing. Every time I speak my mind, one of you tell me that I'm wrong for feeling how I'm feeling. How am I wrong?"

She stood in the middle of the floor and looked back and forth between each person in the room. Nobody seemed to have any more words for her, so she just grabbed her jacket to leave.

"I don't have to deal with this bullshit," she mumbled as she headed for the front door.

When she opened the front door, she was surprised to see someone standing there. The girl at the door was dripping wet from being out in the rain. Her hair was matted to her head, and she looked lost and confused.

"Oh, I was just about to knock."

A young woman that didn't look much older than her stood in front of her. She didn't recognize her to be anyone that she had ever seen before.

"Who are you?" Tamika asked her.

"You don't know me. We've never met, and I don't know any of your friends, but I have seen you all before."

When Candice didn't hear the front door close behind Tamika, she went to see what was taking her so long to leave.

"Who the hell is she?" Candice asked when she saw the little girl standing on Jasmine's front porch.

"I'm still trying to find out," Tamika told her.

"Well, who are you?" Tamika asked her again.

"This is going to be very bad, but I'm coming forward to help your friend, Jasmine. I have to help her."

"Last time, who the fuck are you, and how do you know us?" Candice was losing her patience with the girl.

"Oh my God. What is that bitch doing here?" Jasmine yelled while standing in the hallway. Nobody heard her get out of the bed. Before she got up, Jenna had already entered the living room to see what was going on, so nobody was left in the bedroom to watch Jasmine.

Jasmine ran toward the front door like a crazy woman. The pain from her stitches didn't even matter anymore. She wanted to get to the girl at the door as fast as she could.

Jenna jumped in front of her to stop her from attacking the young woman. She was able to get her to sit down on

49

the couch while everybody else tried to get to the bottom of why the girl was there in the first place.

"Jasmine, this girl says that she can help you," Tamika said.

"Do you guys know who that is?" Jasmine asked still huffing and puffing, trying to catch her breath from running down the hall.

Tamika, Candice, and Jenna all looked at each other as if asking each other if they had any idea who the girl was.

"That is the bitch that kidnapped my baby while we were in the hospital. This bitch left my child on a filthy bathroom floor," Jasmine managed to get out in between breaths. She remembered her face from the photos that the nurses showed her after the incident.

Instantly, Tamika drew her arm back and punched the girl right in her face. Her reaction was so quick that nobody saw it coming.

"You have the nerve to show your face here after what you have done?" Tamika stood over her while she laid down on the porch.

"Please, just hear me out," the girl said while holding

her nose. It had already started bleeding.

"Tamika, let her get up. I want to know how she can help us now," Jenna said, trying to be the voice of reason.

Everybody stepped back while she got back up on her feet. Jenna handed her a paper towel that she got from the kitchen so that she wouldn't drip blood everywhere.

"Come on in, and sit down," Jenna told her.

"Sit down? Did you just invite this bitch into my house? The bitch that kidnapped my newborn son? You bitches are being real damn forgiving," Jasmine spat.

"Listen, my name is Stacey. Yes, I did attempt to kidnap your son, and I am so sorry for that. There is not anything that I can say to make you feel better about that I know. I did it, and it was wrong. I was asked by your baby's father, Corey, to take the baby for him, and I tried but couldn't go through with it. I am a mother, and I would lose my mind if that had happened to me."

"Okay, cut to the fucking chase because I should be calling the police to come haul your ass off to jail." Jasmine was tired of hearing her voice and tired of hearing her apologize.

"Jasmine, I know where your son is… or at least where Corey planned on taking him," Stacey spoke.

Everybody in the room gave her their undivided attention.

"Corey didn't have a plan put in place before he came over here and took your son, but he called me, not knowing what to do when he finally got him. He said that he just came over here because he was mad about the fact that he knew that he would never be able to see him, and he didn't want you to take the baby away from him forever."

"When I talked to him on the phone, I told him to take the baby back to his house, but he refused. He said that he knew that would be the first place you would look, so he couldn't go there."

"Well, where did he go with my baby?" Jasmine blurted out.

"The only places I can think of him going is to the riverfront or some lil' spot on the Southside. I don't know much about the place on the Southside. He just recently started talking about it."

Candice broke away from the group and called

Anthony, but he didn't answer.

"Where the hell are you at, bro?"Candice spoke aloud to no one in particular.

She called his phone again, and once again, she got no answer.

She walked back and forth across the floor in Jasmine's bedroom wondering what to do next. She didn't want to tell Jasmine that she couldn't get Anthony on the phone because she knew that she would worry about him and if he was okay.

"Tamika, come with me," she instructed as she put her jacket on and headed for the door.

"Jenna, stay with Jasmine, and Stacey you don't go anywhere."

Candice and Tamika hopped in her car and headed toward downtown St. Louis. She wasn't sure exactly where she was going or what she was going to find when she got there, but she couldn't just sit in the house and not know what was going on. Plus, she couldn't get Anthony on the phone for him to give her an update on his whereabouts.

Her mind was racing thinking about where Malcolm

was. It was cold outside, and the rain just began to fall. She knew that wherever he was he was just out there with nothing. Corey's dumb ass didn't even take the baby's diaper bag when he left.

"God, please guide me through these streets. Please, send me in the direction to find this baby," Candice spoke aloud.

Tamika didn't say anything. She just looked at Candice and noticed the worry on her face. She knew that everybody was concerned about Malcolm's whereabouts, and she was too. She knew that Corey was crazy, and she wasn't sure how crazy.

Candice was looking through her windshield wipers at every intersection and highway ramp she passed going down Highway 70, hoping to spot them, but she never did.

Tamika felt her phone vibrate. When she looked at the screen to check the caller ID, it was Jasmine. She contemplated if she should answer it or not because she didn't have any news to tell her yet. She looked over at Candice, who wasn't paying her any attention.

"What's up, Jay?" Tamika asked after she put her

phone on speaker phone so that Candice could hear the conversation too.

"Anthony and DeAndre found Corey," she said through tears.

"Where are they?" Candice asked.

"On the East Side at Corey's baby's mama's house,"

"Is Malcolm okay?"

"I don't know. Anthony wouldn't tell me anything over the phone. He did say that it didn't take them long to find him though. Once they spotted his car, they stayed on his ass until he stopped. I guess he ran out of places to go, so he went over the bridge."

"Candice, please go get my baby."

"I'm headed to where they are now."

Tamika ended the call and stared out of her window. "Do you know where this girl lives?" she asked Candice.

"Yeah, I had to go over there with Jasmine a few times."

Not knowing what she was going to be walking into, Candice checked her center console for her pistol. After locating it, she sat it on her lap and continued to where the guys were at.

"Tamika, you know you could be a little more supportive. Jasmine needs us right now. What if someone took your baby twice and you had no idea where your newborn child was, how would you feel?"

"I don't know Candice because I don't have kids, but I can imagine it being very scary."

"I don't have kids either, but it's just a matter of being compassionate for someone that you know is hurting," Candice pressed.

"I'm really not up for this conversation right now, Candice. Save me the tongue lashing."

"You're right. You're shole right. Just hope that you are not ever in a position where you need somebody to be there for you."

Tamika didn't say anything. She just rolled her eyes and continued looking out of her window.

When Candice pulled up in front of Corey's baby's mama's house, she saw Anthony and DeAndre outside on the front lawn. They were saying something to Corey, but she didn't know what. Corey was standing on the front lawn holding baby Malcolm like a football tucked under his arm. Malcolm was crying, and everyone had their guns drawn.

"Get back, C!" DeAndre yelled at Candice when she got out of her car. Corey's baby's mom was on the front porch, calling out to Corey to put his gun down and to hand Malcolm over to Anthony, but the more she talked the more frustrated he became.

"Bitch, shut up, and go in the house!" he yelled back at her. He went to her because he thought that she would help him hide Malcolm until he could figure out what his next move would be, but when he found out she wasn't willing to participate in his shenanigans, he went back outside, and that's when he was met by Anthony and DeAndre.

She was crying, and Malcolm was crying. It was dark, cold, and rainy. Candice knew that he was a nigga on the edge because he kept pointing his gun at himself and then at Malcolm. Anthony wanted to just shoot his ass, but he didn't know how much of a risk that would be for the baby.

"Look, if I can't have my son, then no one can have my son." Corey broke down in tears.

Corey pointed his gun at Malcolm again and before he could pull the trigger he hit the ground, and his son fell right beside him.

Everything and everyone became still. It seemed as though Corey fell in slow motion, and once he hit the ground, nothing else moved.

Everybody looked around to see who pulled the trigger. When Anthony's eyes met Candice's, he knew that it was her.

Corey's baby's mama let out the most horrifying scream, and that's what broke the silence. Candice was still frozen in the same spot with her gun drawn. Tamika ran over to assess Malcolm's condition, and DeAndre walked over to Candice.

"Are you okay?" he asked her.

"Somebody had to do it," she replied in a shaky voice.

DeAndre took the gun from Candice, placed it in the waistband of his pants, and sat her down on the passenger side of her car.

He went over to where Tamika was with the baby. "How is he?"

"He seems to be fine. Just cold," she answered while rocking him. She had wrapped him up in the bottom of her shirt for extra warmth.

"Go sit in my car and turn the heat on so he can warm up," Anthony told Tamika.

Anthony walked over to where Corey laid on the grass in the front yard and checked him for a pulse. His baby's mama was lying on top of him, still crying and screaming.

"He's gone y'all," Anthony announced.

Candice dropped her head as she began to feel a little bit of guilt for taking someone's life, but she knew that it had to be her to do it. She knew that if Anthony did it, he would have to face the law. If he went to jail, it would crush Jasmine. She needed him free to protect her and their son. Everybody looked at each other when they heard sirens blaring in the distance. They knew that they were headed in their direction, so they had to think fast. Everybody's first mind was to just get in their cars and head to Jasmine's place, but they knew that Corey's baby's mama was going tell what happened. They all weren't going to get away that easily.

Candice told Anthony, DeAndre, and Tamika to go back to Jasmine's house, and she'd stay and talk to the police.

"I'll stay with her. Everybody else can go," DeAndre said.

"DeAndre, please go. I shot Corey. I don't want anybody else involved in this," Candice pleaded.

"I'm here. You don't have to face this alone."

Anthony kept baby Malcolm wrapped up and handed him over to Tamika. They jumped in his car and sped off.

DeAndre wrapped his arm around Candice's shoulders and told her that everything was going to be okay. He wasn't so sure of it, but he wanted to comfort her the best way he could.

"He was a bad man, but did he deserve to die?" Candice questioned as she watched his daughter standing at the screen door of the house. She was using her little finger to scribble through the fog that covered the screen door while her mother sat out on the front lawn holding her lifeless father in her arms.

"Look at her Dre. She's so innocent, she doesn't even

know what's going on, and I took her father from her. I deserve to go to jail. How can I live the rest of my life knowing the kind of pain that I have caused and be okay with that?

"Candice you did what you had to do. Do not beat yourself up over this. You saved your best friend's baby, and he can no longer hurt either of them again."

"But I'm not a killer, Dre!" Candice broke out in tears as the guilt began to take over. She couldn't believe what she had done.

"Shh, shh, shh, pull it together," DeAndre told her as the police arrived on the scene.

The husky white man in uniform didn't seem too interested in the situation. He took names, phone numbers, and statements from Candice, DeAndre, and Corey's baby's mama.

When he asked who was responsible for Corey's murder, his baby mama told them that it was a random shooting. She told them that they were all just sitting outside talking and a random guy walked through the crowd and targeted Corey.

She explained to the officer that she had never seen the guy before, and she gave him a false description of the person. She let him know that she didn't know of any extracurricular activities that Corey could have been involved in that would make somebody want to hurt him. She was hoping that no one else saw what really happened because she didn't want them to come back with more questions that she would have to lie about later.

Candice's eyes grew large when she heard the lie just flow out of the girl's mouth. She knew for sure that she was about to have to face time for murdering Corey in cold blood, with witnesses.

DeAndre was shocked as well. He held Candice a little bit tighter when the officer asked them who was responsible because he knew that she was going to confess. She was shaking and holding back tears. She was slowly breaking, and he knew that she would not be able to lie about it, so he was relieved to hear Corey's baby's mom shoot the cop her bogus story.

The officer promised to find out who killed Corey, gave everybody one of his business cards, and went to speak to the other officers and first responders as they arrived on the scene.

"Hey, you didn't have to do that, man," DeAndre told Corey's baby's mom.

"Corey wasn't always a bad person. He used to be a really good guy. I don't know what happened to him that made him change, but you saw me many days beaten and bruised when you and he hung out. You witnessed, first hand, how he spoke to me and how bad he treated me. I know exactly what he put that other girl through, and now this crazy shit with this baby... He had it coming, Dre. Somebody was going to fuck his ass up eventually," she said after standing up and getting close enough to DeAndre that nobody around them would be able to hear.

"I know, but I appreciate it still because you didn't have to."

DeAndre saw the hurt in her eyes, but nobody wanted it to end like it did. Corey just didn't know when or how to stop.

When the police officers allowed everyone to leave, Corey's baby's mother walked over to Candice and gave her a hug. She saw that she was torn up about everything, and she was too, but she just expected it to happen sooner or later.

"Shake it off, baby girl. Don't let this consume you," she whispered into Candice's ear before breaking the embrace.

DeAndre walked Candice over to her car.

"Give me the keys, C."

Still in a fog, she handed her car keys over to DeAndre. He motioned for her to come over and sit down in her driver's seat. When she did, he kneeled down next to her and whispered.

"I know you are shook up right now, but I need you to pull it together long enough to get back to Jasmine's house. Can you do that?" he asked.

She nodded her head.

"I'm going to drive Anthony's car back. I would drive you, but I can't leave the car here. The police will run his plates and trace the car to him, and they'll know that he was here. Just follow me."

DeAndre reached over her and pulled the seatbelt

across Candice's chest and secured it.

"C, you gotta snap out of it, baby. It's going to be alright. I promise."

DeAndre hopped in Anthony's car that Corey drove over there and pulled off. He headed back across the bridge. He wanted to get back to his neck of the woods as soon as possible. He hated the East Side. If he wasn't going over there for the nightlife, he wasn't messing with it.

He turned the radio on, adjusted his seat, and checked his rearview mirror to make sure Candice was following him.

CHAPTER FIVE

When Anthony pulled up in front of Jasmine's apartment building, he looked over at Tamika holding Malcolm.

"Are you ready to take him in?"

Malcolm had cried most of the ride back home. Anthony knew that he was hungry, but he didn't have anything to give since he was a breastfed baby. Eventually, a little rocking from Tamika and the car ride lulled him to sleep.

"Let's go. He needs his mom," Tamika told him.

They both stepped out of the car and headed up the steps. They expected to be bombarded when they walked in with the baby, but the only person there was Jenna.

"Where's Jasmine?" Anthony asked her.

"She's in the bed. I gave her some of her pain medication, a cup of tea, and made her lie down. She was too upset. She was just hurting herself."

"He hasn't been hurt has he?" Jenna questioned.

"No, not that we can see," Tamika told her.

"Man, you guys are soaking wet. It looks like y'all were out fighting in the rain."

Jenna went into the linen closet and grabbed a bunch of towels for them to dry off and wipe the water off the floors.

Anthony walked back into his and Jasmine's bedroom to check on her.

"Jay, baby, Malcolm's home," he whispered in her ear before kissing her on her forehead. He was hoping that she'd wake up, but she didn't.

He walked back out of the bedroom with some clothes for Malcolm. He handed them to Tamika and let her dry him off and dress him.

After the baby was cleaned up, Tamika went and grabbed a pair of Jasmine's sweatpants and a t-shirt out of her closet to slip on. She couldn't sit around in her wet clothes, and she knew that Jasmine wouldn't mind.

Anthony stepped out of the room and called DeAndre's cell phone. After about three rings, it went to voicemail.

He began to get antsy. He wanted to know what was going on. He didn't know if he and Candice were still in

East St. Louis or if they were being detained or anything.

He went back into the living room with the girls and the baby. He figured he'd give it a few minutes to see if DeAndre called him back.

"So what happened? Where did you find Malcolm?" Jenna asked as she held him and gently stroked his baby hair.

"Girl. it's such a long story," Tamika told her.

"Well, that's what I'm here for," she replied.

Before Tamika could say anything, the front door flew open.

Candice walked in first. She didn't say anything to anybody. She was covering her mouth with her hands and ran to the bathroom.

Anthony was about to go after her to see what was wrong with her, but DeAndre was right behind her.

"I got it, Ant," DeAndre said, stopping Anthony from following her.

Anthony stopped in his tracks and let DeAndre handle it.

Everyone in the living room could hear Candice

throwing up.

"What's wrong with her?" Jenna frowned up at the sounds that were coming out of the bathroom.

Tamika got up and walked into Jasmine's room and grabbed the clothes that she had picked out for Candice. She knew that if she made it back there, she would need something to change into.

"What is all of that noise?" Jasmine asked as she began to slowly come to.

"Candice is in the bathroom throwing up."

When she realized that it was Tamika talking to her and not Jenna, she sat straight up on the bed.

"Where's Malcolm?" she asked with her eyes wide and a heart full of hope for some good news.

"He's in the living room with the others," Tamika dryly replied.

Tamika walked out of the room and opened the bathroom door where she found Candice leaning over the toilet and DeAndre holding her hair out of the way. She threw the clothes on the floor next to where Candice sat and told them that they were for her to change into.

"Jasmine is awake, y'all," Tamika told the gang when she walked into the living room.

Anthony jumped to his feet and immediately went to her bedside.

"Hey, baby. Are you okay?" Jasmine asked when she saw him walk into the room. She sat up and rubbed the side of his face.

"I'm fine. How are you, baby?" he asked as he brushed her hair out of her face.

"I'm so happy to see you, Anthony. I was going crazy worrying about you and Malcolm. Where is he?"

"He's in the living room with everybody. He's sleeping right now."

"Was he hurt?"

"No, baby. He's fine. I can go get him for you. I know he's hungry."

"No, if he's sleeping, then let him rest. I'm just happy that you two are alright."

"Where did you find him?"

"I caught up with Corey at his baby's mom's house."

"He took my baby all the way to the East Side?" she

asked in a high pitched tone.

"I have something to tell you," Anthony's voice was serious, and his face was straight.

"What is it?" she asked, noticing the look on his face.

"Corey is dead, Jas." Anthony focused his eyes on her and waited for her reaction. He didn't know what to expect.

"You killed him?" she asked.

"I didn't kill him, Jas. Candice did."

Jasmine's eyes grew wide. She was completely shocked at what she had just heard.

Candice ain't no killer, she thought to herself.

"How the hell did Candice kill Corey? Are you sure it was her?"

"Babe, Candice shot him. He had his gun out, and he kept pointing it back and forth between him and Malcolm. Everyone had their guns drawn ready to take a shot but didn't want to because we didn't know if it would cause him to shoot Malcolm. I guess she got tired of waiting, so when he pointed the gun back at himself, she took her shot."

"Why is she in the bathroom throwing up, though?"

"She killed a man. She's sick to her stomach. It's fucking with her real bad right now."

"Damn," was all Jasmine could say. She put her head down, and quickly, visions of Corey and some of the times that they've spent together ran through her mind. Over the last few years, they shared so many moments that were good and bad, but now, she hated his guts, but she didn't want him to have to die because of it.

She hated the fact that her son would never get to know his biological father. She never wanted that. He wasn't the greatest person, but he did have some good things about him that she would have wanted him to know. She always hoped that one day he would get himself together so that he could have a relationship with his son. She already knew that he loved his daughter to death. But now, their son would never get the chance to know his father other than what people would tell him about him when he was old enough to understand.

Anthony noticed her mood change with the news she had just gotten.

"Everything is going to be okay, baby. We have so

many great things to look forward to right now. When all of this passes, we will be able to focus on them. At least you don't have to worry about him bothering you or Malcolm anymore."

"I guess you're right, but it still hurts a little," Jasmine expressed.

DeAndre emerged from the bathroom, giving Candice some privacy to change into the clothes that Tamika had given her. Before he could make it into the living room with everyone else, Anthony walked up to him in the hallway.

"Hey, man, let me talk to you real quick," Anthony told him, leading him to the back of the apartment where the balcony was.

"What's up?" DeAndre asked him.

"What happened when the police showed up? I wasn't sure if Candice was going to make it back here. I just knew for sure that she was going to jail tonight."

"You won't believe this. Corey's baby's mom covered for her. She gave the police a bogus story about how Corey got shot. Me and Candice were shocked too. You know

Candice was all ready to confess, but ol' girl stepped up and put it off on somebody else."

"Damn. That's what's up. When all of this blows over, I might get at her and break her off a few racks or something for helping her out like that."

"She was saying that she knew how Corey was out in these streets trippin' on everybody and shit, and she knew that somebody was bound to get him sooner or later."

"I'm just glad that she didn't snitch, though. That shit just would have brought us more problems and cost us more money in the long run," Anthony whispered.

"Does Jasmine know what happened. Does she know that Corey is dead?" DeAndre asked.

"Yeah, she knows. I told her. She took it okay, I guess."

"That's what's up."

"Let's get back inside. It's cold as hell out here," Anthony told DeAndre.

When the guys went back in the house, everybody was in the living room chatting. Anthony overheard Candice asking Jenna and Jasmine where Stacey went.

"She left. I tried to keep her here, but she left," Jenna

confessed.

"I told that lil' bitch to stay here," Candice replied

"Who is Stacey?" Anthony asked.

"The girl from the hospital. The one that tried to kidnap Malcolm," Jasmine spoke up.

"She was here?" Anthony asked in confusion.

"Yeah, she just showed up on our doorstep after you left. I don't even know how she knew where we lived, but she said that she could help us find Corey and Malcolm. Although all the places that she told us were false."

"Yeah, the lil' bitch came over here all apologetic about what she did, talking about she wanted to help us find them because she is a mother, and she didn't know what she would do if someone did that to her," Candice said.

"Tamika punched the poor girl in her face," Jenna said, laughing.

Just the thought of it made Candice and Jasmine laugh too.

"It's too much going on. Random mothafuckas poppin' up at the crib and shit. Crazy niggas breaking into the crib while we are here. People are getting too bold, and I feel like I'm slippin. I'm supposed to be able to protect my family, and that ain't happening," Anthony voiced loudly.

"So what do you suggest we do, Anthony?" Jasmine asked.

"I think it's time you finally take me up on my offer to move. You have been here long enough. I've been trying to get you to move for a long time now, and you keep turning me down, but I have a place that's safer for you and Malcolm."

"We can make this place safer, Anthony. This is my home. This is where I'm comfortable. If Corey's dead, who else do I have to worry about?"

"I don't want you and the baby to stay here long enough to find out."

For a minute, nobody said anything. Everybody just looked back and forth between Jasmine and Anthony, depending on who was talking.

"Where is the house you're talking about, Anthony?" Jenna asked.

"I got a spot over in Ladue. It'll be a whole lot safer

than here. I can buy you out of your lease and have you moved in a few days."

Jasmine looked around at all of her friends. Although no one voiced their opinions on the situation, she could see the looks on their faces and knew that they were on his side with this one.

"Well, I guess it's settled. I'll be moving out of here sooner than later."

"I don't want anyone other than you all to know where Jasmine is, so I don't want to hire a moving company. Can you ladies help her get everything packed up? When you are finished, DeAndre and I can move the furniture. I'll get a few more guys to help us."

"I'm here to help." DeAndre stepped up.

"I can help," Jenna spoke up.

"You know I'm here," Candice replied.

"I'll be here. Just let me know when," Tamika said.

"Cool. I'll tell y'all when in a few days. I'll make this payment to the landlord tomorrow."

Malcolm began to whine a little bit, so Jenna handed him over to Jasmine. She excused herself from the group and went to her bedroom to change his diaper and breastfeed him in private.

"I know it's late, y'all. I ain't putting y'all out, but I'm heading to the back. If y'all wanna stay, you know where the blankets are. If you leave, just let somebody know so they can lock up behind you," Anthony told everybody.

"I'll go ahead and leave now. I have work in a few hours," Tamika said as she stood up.

"Yeah, I'm out too," Jenna said.

"I'll stay a little while longer," Candice responded.

"I'll stay with her to make sure she's okay," DeAndre said.

Jenna and Tamika peeked around the corner of the bedroom door and said their goodbyes to Jasmine. They didn't go all the way in because they didn't want to disturb the baby from his feeding.

"Alright, y'all, we'll get up with you later," Anthony said as he stood on the front porch and watched Jenna and Tamika get to their cars safely.

"It's after two already," DeAndre said, looking at his cell phone.

"I know, bro. I'm beat," Anthony replied with a yawn.

He checked the windows throughout the apartment to make sure that everything was locked, and he was sure to lock the front door. He closed the blinds and turned off lights that weren't being used.

"If y'all decide to leave in the middle of the night, come and let me know so I can lock the door."

DeAndre nodded in agreement, and Candice said her goodnight to Anthony. She got up so that she could tell Jasmine goodnight and kiss the baby. When she went back into the living room, DeAndre was sitting on the floor in front of the couch.

"I left the couch open so that you could lie down."

"I'm good. I think I'm going to sit over here and see what's on TV."

Candice sat down in a chair and channel surfed until she found something.

"What's this?" DeAndre asked.

"*Almost Christmas.* You mean to tell me you've never seen this movie before?"

"If it's a chick flick, I ain't seen it. Now movies with

Bruce Lee or some gangsta shit, I've probably seen them all. If I ain't got no girlfriend, it ain't no reason for me to be sitting up watching a girlie movie."

"Boy, you trippin. It's so many movies out that are not gangsta movies or fighting movies that are really good. You missing out, Dre."

"I'll take your word for it."

"If you put your phone down long enough to watch it, you might find out how good it is."

"It sounds like you are trying to boss me around, but since you are my peeps, I'll let you get away with it," DeAndre teased.

Candice found a comfortable volume and sat the remote down on an end table that was sitting in between the couch and the chair that she was sitting in. She turned sideways to drape her legs over the side of the chair.

"Candice, you can lay on the couch. You don't have to be uncomfortable in the chair."

"Then, where are you going to sleep? Besides, I'll be getting up to leave after this movie anyway, so I don't need to get too comfortable so that I can get up."

80

"Don't worry about me. I'll be fine," DeAndre told her.

Candice blew him off and continued to watch the movie. She didn't want to continue having a conversation about who was going to sleep and where she was good.

Eventually, DeAndre found himself laughing at some of the scenes of the movie. At least the ones that he could catch in between matching the candy on Candy Crush on his cell phone.

Candice caught him laughing at some parts.

"Oh yeah, chick flick, huh?" she teased.

"It's cool. The movie is funny, so what?"

About ten minutes passed, and DeAndre hadn't heard a word or laughter from Candice. He looked over to where she was sitting to find her asleep.

"I told her ass to get on the couch so she could stretch out," he mumbled to himself. He got up off the floor, picked her up, and carried her over to the couch. As soon as her body hit the couch she turned over with her back to DeAndre. He went and grabbed a blanket out of the linen closet and covered her up.

DeAndre sat over in the chair that he took Candice out

of and finished watching the movie that she turned on. He couldn't deny the movie turned out to be a good one. When the movie went off, he turned the TV off instead of finding something else to watch. He wanted to get a few hours of sleep so that he'd be ready for whatever was going to jump off later on that day.

It seemed like as soon as he dozed off, he was startled out of his sleep. He kept hearing Candice talking in her sleep. He didn't bother her at first; he just sat there and listened to what she was saying.

He realized that she was having a bad dream when she started saying "no" over and over again. At some point, it looked like she was fighting someone in her sleep.

He walked over to her and tried to wake her up, but she wouldn't.

"C, wake up. Candice, get up, baby," he said as he leaned in closer to her.

She jumped when she saw him standing over her. She got up and ran to the bathroom. DeAndre followed closely behind her.

"C, what's wrong?" he asked with concern.

She couldn't speak. She just went straight to the toilet and started throwing up just like she did earlier that day.

"Is she okay? I heard some commotion, so I got up to see what it was," Anthony said, peeking his head in the bathroom.

"She was having a bad dream and then woke up and ran in here. I guess she's still sick about everything that's happened," DeAndre answered while holding Candice's hair back just like he had before.

Anthony walked away from the bathroom and came back with a washcloth and a cup of crushed ice.

"Here, put some cool water on this and wipe her face and around her neck. Let her suck on this ice when she's done. It might help her keep all that down. There are crackers in the kitchen if she wants those too."

"Alright, fam. Thanks, man," DeAndre replied to Anthony's hospitality.

"Do you need me to stay up with y'all?"

"Naw, man. We'll be fine. Go get some rest."

Without a word, Anthony turned around and headed back to his bedroom. He was sleep before he knew it. The day had been so hard and hectic for everybody. They all were exhausted, and with Candice being sick, it didn't look like she and DeAndre would be getting any rest anytime soon.

"Dre, you really don't have to take care of me. I'll be alright. If I was at home by myself, I would be taking care of myself anyway," Candice told him when she stood up to wash her hands and clean herself up.

"But you're not at home, and you're not by yourself. I'm here. I don't mind helping you."

Candice shook her head and continued doing what she was doing. She took the washcloth that Anthony sat on the counter, ran some lukewarm water on it, and rung it out. She looked over at DeAndre that was sitting on the edge of the bathtub watching her.

"DeAndre, how long are you going to sit there and watch me?"

"Damn, C. I'll go back into the living room if I'm bothering you." He was annoyed that she was annoyed by him when all he wanted to do was help and support her.

He got up and went to sit back down in the living room.

He checked the time on his cell phone and noted that it was almost four in the morning.

Candice couldn't believe that DeAndre had gotten upset because she said something to him about him watching her. She blew it off and wiped her face and neck as Anthony suggested. She also took the bottle of mouthwash that was on the counter and poured some into her mouth to gargle the throw up taste out of her mouth.

When she was finished, she grabbed her cup of ice and went back into the living room to find DeAndre sitting in the chair. He appeared to be asleep.

"Boy, get up. I know you ain't sleep that fast," she said, nudging his arm.

He didn't move.

"DeAndre, get up. Quit playing," she said, hitting him with a pillow.

"C, stop hitting me, man," he told her, obviously in his feelings.

"What's your problem?"

"I ain't got no problem. What's yours?"

"I got to have a problem because I didn't want you

sitting there staring at me?"

"No, you have a problem because y'all women always yapping about men don't do this and men don't do that and men ain't supportive or whatever, and as soon as one is, it's something wrong with it. I swear, women are some confusing ass creatures. It doesn't matter the color, the nationality, the age, all of y'all are confusing as hell."

"He's right, C," Anthony cosigned while walking past them to go into the kitchen.

"That's some bull. Ain't you supposed to be sleep?" she asked Anthony.

"I was, I'm going back, but what he said is still right," he said, walking back to the bedroom.

Candice and DeAndre laughed at Anthony as he continued his conversation but never stopped walking.

"Look, if it's that big of a deal to you, I wasn't upset about you watching me. It was just kind of awkward. With the kind of night I've had and now morning, I don't want anybody looking at me."

"It's cool. Just remember I've been with you every step of the way. You weren't alone, and you don't have to be.

You do have support," he spoke sincerely.

"I appreciate it," was all she said.

Candice held her hands out in front of her for DeAndre to grab. When he did, she pulled him out of the chair he was sitting in and pulled him in for a hug.

"Thanks for being my friend," she whispered in his ear.

"Anytime, C," he replied.

She pulled him over to the couch and sat him down first. With his back against the arm of the couch and one leg on the back of the couch, she sat down in between his legs. She rested her back against his chest and allowed him to hold her until she fell asleep again.

CHAPTER SIX

"Look at this," Jasmine said, stopping Anthony in the hallway of their apartment.

When she woke up to change and feed Malcolm, she saw Candice and DeAndre lying on the couch together.

"I'm glad they finally went to sleep. They were up bickering all night. If I didn't know any better, I would have thought they were an old married couple," Anthony joked.

"I heard that," DeAndre said, wiping his eyes.

"Well, I ain't lying."

DeAndre rubbed Candice's arms in an attempt to gently wake her up.

When she did open her eyes, she looked around the room like she didn't know where she was. Then, she saw Anthony and Jasmine looking at her.

"What y'all looking at? Y'all act like y'all ain't never seen somebody sleep before."

"Naw, we ain't never seen y'all two sleep together before."

"Y'all trippin', making a big deal out of nothing."

Candice looked back at DeAndre who was looking at her. She smiled and pulled his arms around her even tighter.

"Just five more minutes," she said before closing her eyes again.

Jasmine laughed at her best friend. If she didn't know any better, she would think that her girl was catching feelings for their homeboy.

Normally, Candice would have been up panicking about being late for work, but she figured she'd just take a sick day or maybe a sick week. She just wasn't feeling it.

When Jasmine finished feeding Malcolm, she handed him over to Anthony to burp and entertain him while she started breakfast. Candice got up to help her.

"What's going on with you two?" Jasmine inquired, nodding her head toward DeAndre, who was still sitting in the living room.

"Nothing is going on. He's just been trying to help me get through the incident that took place the other night. He's been adamant about supporting me through it, so I gave in and let him."

"That's what's up. He's always been such a sweet guy and a good friend," Jasmine told her.

When the food was done, the girls called the guys into the kitchen. Anthony came in with the baby. He sat him down in his rocker.

"Do you guys need help with anything?" DeAndre asked when he walked into the kitchen.

"No, we just need you to take a seat."

DeAndre sat down and looked at all of the food on the table. His stomach was growling loudly. He was ready to get his grub on.

There were scrambled eggs with cheese, crispy bacon, pancakes, sausages, fried potatoes, grits, buttered biscuits, toast, a fruit tray, orange juice, and milk.

"You women must have woke up feeling really good to be feeding us like this," Anthony said while scooping food onto his plate.

"I just felt like cooking. That's all," Jasmine said.

"Well, everything looks good," Anthony said and leaned over to kiss her.

"Come on, y'all, not at the table," Candice teased.

For the most part, everyone sat quietly while they ate their breakfast, just chiming in every now and then to comment on how good the food was. Everybody's mind was consumed with the events of the last few hours.

When Anthony was done eating, he didn't stay to make small talk. He got up from the table and placed his plate, fork, and glass in the sink.

"That was delicious, ladies. Thank you."

"Where are you going?" Jasmine asked.

"I have to go talk to your landlord about breaking your lease here. I'm ready to get that cracking so we can get you moved out of here."

Jasmine didn't say anything else. She just rolled her eyes and took a sip of her orange juice. She was not thrilled about having to move. She felt like she was being forced out of the place she'd grown comfortable in over the last few years. Although when she looked around and thought about all of the bad things that happened in that apartment, a fresh start didn't seem too bad after all.

She was able to look around and remember the exact

spot in each room where Corey had violated her—the wall that she was pushed against and choked out on when Jenna was at her home to witness the abuse for the first time, and the bathroom where she spent countless hours covering her face with makeup to hide the bruises that Corey put on her.

Yeah, maybe it is time to go, she thought to herself.

Jasmine got up from the table and started clearing away the empty dishes that once had food on them. She walked over to the sink to rinse them out before loading her dishwasher.

"Jay, I'll do that. Go get some rest. Have you taken your medicine today?" Candice asked her.

"That's the only way I'm up on my feet." She laughed.

"Well, go sit down, boo. I got this."

When Jasmine walked out of the kitchen, Candice sat back down to finish her food.

"So, how are you doing, C?" DeAndre asked her.

"I'm good."

"No, how are you *really* doing?" he pushed.

Candice pushed her chair away from the table and stood up. She took her dirty dishes to the sink and finished clearing the table of the things that Jasmine didn't get.

After rinsing the dishes, she turned around to face DeAndre.

"Do you think the detectives are going to find out that I was the one that shot Corey?"

DeAndre could hear the concern in her voice. He walked over to her and pulled her in for a hug.

"C, I think everything is going to be okay, and whatever happens, you got us. We are all here for you."

"I'm scared, Dre. I didn't want to kill him. I just didn't want him to hurt Malcolm," she confessed. She could no longer fight back the tears that she had been holding in.

DeAndre lifted her head so they could see eye to eye. He wiped the tears from her face.

"I promise you... you're going to be alright. Everything is going to work out the way it should."

Candice lowered her head back onto his chest and continued to cry.

He lifted her head again and kissed her through her tears.

Candice froze. She wasn't sure about how she should

feel about DeAndre's kiss. That was something that has never happened before. They'd always been only friends.

Hearing Malcolm start to fuss snapped her out of her thoughts. She immediately broke out of DeAndre's embrace.

"Hey, C, I'm sorry. I crossed the line," he told her. He noticed that she seemed a bit apprehensive.

"It's cool," she replied before picking up the baby and walking out of the kitchen.

DeAndre finished cleaning up the kitchen so that the girls wouldn't have to do it. He couldn't get Candice off of his mind. He was feeling her a little bit, but he never expected to kiss her. That came as a surprise to him as well. When he was done, he went to Jasmine's bedroom to say his goodbyes.

"I have some things to take care of. I'll check in with y'all later. Call my cell if you need anything," he told them, standing in the doorway. He and Candice locked eyes but no words were exchanged.

"Okay, Dre. Thanks for everything," Jasmine spoke up.

When Candice and Jasmine heard the front door close, Candice went to the door to make sure it was locked.

When she saw him pull off, she walked back into the bedroom with Jasmine.

"What was that all about?" Jasmine asked.

"What you mean?"

"Don't play crazy with me, Candice. It's something going on with you and DeAndre."

"There's nothing going on, Jay. I just think I may be feeling him a little bit."

Jasmine's face lit up, and a big smile spread across her lips.

"I knew something was up, but I just didn't know what. Hell, I knew it when I woke up and saw you all wrapped up in his arms."

"Yeah, that shocked the hell out of me too. You know I don't let people get that close to me. Ever since the incident with Corey back at the warehouse, I've seen a different side of him. And then within the last day, he's been so supportive. It's kind of hard to reject him," Candice revealed.

"He is a really sweet guy. I say if it makes you happy, go for it. I know y'all are friends and have been for a long time, but maybe it's time to let him out the friend zone and see what things could really be like."

"But wouldn't that be weird? He was shooting for you first."

"It wouldn't be weird for me. It is what it is, and it wasn't meant to be with me and Dre. It might be what's meant for you."

"I'll think about it, but it's not something that I want to rush into."

"Sounds good."

"I'm going to go home so that I can get cleaned up. When I wash these clothes, I'll make sure I get them back to you. Do you need anything before I leave?"

"Naw, I'll be fine. Once I take my medicine, I'll be able to move around a little bit more. I know that I have you, Anthony, and DeAndre on standby. I'll call one of you if I need anything."

Candice stood up and kissed Jasmine on her cheek and did the same to Malcolm before leaving. She turned the lock on the doorknob and went on her way.

CHAPTER SEVEN

The news of Corey being shot and killed hurt Kerry to the core. He knew that his twin brother was foul and did some real dirty things, but he didn't think that death was the answer. He would rather see his brother in jail than in a casket.

He didn't know how he was going to be able to go on with the rest of his life without his brother by his side. That was his best friend and always had been. Now, he had nobody. It was just him. He remembered Corey always saying that they came into the world together, and they were going to leave the world together. If only he had been there at the time that he got killed, that probably would have been true.

He promised himself that he would get revenge on whoever killed him. He refused to let that happen, and he did not do anything about it. He kept his ears to the street because he knew the streets would be talking eventually.

In the back of his mind, he thought that Stacey had something to do with it. He knew that Corey and Stacey weren't on the best terms at the moment, and he figured that she was probably mad enough at him to kill him or have him killed. He wanted to believe that Stacey was a good and innocent girl, but the truth was he didn't really know her that well. He didn't know what she was capable of.

Kerry laid on his living room floor, looking up at the ceiling. He let thoughts of his brother consume him. He thought about him from their childhood until now. He wondered if he had been there with his brother at the time that all of this happened, would it have still happened anyway.

After hours of reflection, he finally drifted off into a deep sleep only to wake up confused. This time, his girlfriend was laying on the floor next to him. She managed to creep in while he was still sleeping. When he got up off the floor, she got up too. He ran into Corey's room, looking for his brother, but his brother wasn't there. He thought that he had been dreaming that his brother was dead. He just knew that he would be there.

"Hey, baby, where's Corey?" he asked, rushing back

into the living room.

"I told you. He's gone, baby. He's dead," she answered, wondering why he was flipping out.

"You mean to tell me that Corey is dead? Like… never coming back?" he asked again for clarification. Kerry had been in denial about his brother's death from the first time that he heard about it. It wasn't something that he could just accept so easily.

She walked over to him and put her hands gently on each of his arms.

"He's gone, Kerry," she said it softly but sternly. She wanted him to understand that Corey was not coming back.

Kerry began to sweat profusely and paced his living room floor. His steps got faster and faster. His girlfriend thought that he was going to literally burn a hole in the floor.

She walked over to him and grabbed him to stop him from walking anymore. When he finally stopped, he fell into her arms and cried like a baby. It hit him hard. At some point, he even contemplated suicide, but if he were to go through with it, it wouldn't be before he found his brother's killers. He was going to make them pay for what they had done.

His girlfriend comforted him as long as she could before he got up and punched a hole through the wall in a rage. It wasn't just one punch. He hit the wall several times. He had gotten to a point of fury that frightened her. She was scared to stay there and scared of what he'd do if she left. She knew that he had spoken of suicide since this incident, and she didn't want to leave him alone for him to hurt himself. She walked over to him and showed him the blood that was running down his arms. She suggested that he go take a shower so that she could start dinner. She decided to try a gentle approach. She didn't know what to expect from him. Her heart broke for him. She hated for him to be hurting, and she hated the reason that he was hurting even more. She turned on some music, got dinner started, rolled a blunt, and sat back with her feet up to wait for Kerry to get out of the shower.

That shower must have done the trick because he came out of the shower a whole different person. He was so much calmer. "Hey, bae. I was thinking."

"What's up?"

"You remember that girl Stacey that I was telling you about, the girl that Corey was messing around with?"

"Yeah, what's up with her?"

"Do you think she had something to do with Corey getting killed?"

She thought about the question for a minute, trying to figure out what reason would she have to kill him. As a matter of fact, she knew that Stacey wasn't the one that killed Corey. She couldn't tell him that, but she knew it.

Before she could respond, he continued, "Or maybe his baby mama, Jasmine and her dude. I know they were pissed about him trying to kidnap their baby at that hospital, and I didn't even know about that until way after it happened, but that's more than enough of a motive right there."

"Are those the only people you can think of?"

"I don't know. I'm trying to work this shit out in my head, and I just can't put it together. I gotta plan a funeral. I don't know how to do that. I've never had to bury someone before. The last time I've been to a funeral, I was just a little kid. I don't know how I'm going to see my twin brother in a casket. That's like looking at myself in a casket. I can't do it, T. I can't."

Kerry's girlfriend hit the blunt two times and held it up to his lips. He took it from her and hit it a few times too. She slowly pushed him down on the couch, opened his towel, and straddled him.

"Come on, baby. What are you doing? I'm trying to talk to you about my brother," Kerry pleaded.

"Shhh. Let me take some of this pressure off of you."

She kissed him on his neck and worked her way down to his chest. She let her tongue glide down his body until she reached his penis. He tried to fight her off. Even though it felt so good, he wanted to get to the bottom of his brother's murder.

The more he tried to push her away, the harder she sucked. When she opened her mouth wide and let his dick slide halfway down her throat, his eyes rolled back. She released his dick and stood up to remove her clothes.

She stood in front of him completely naked. He looked over her body in amazement. Every curve was just right.

As she moved closer to him, he sat up and turned her around so that her back was to him. He lifted her to spread her legs apart and sat her right on his dick. When she got comfortable, she rode him until he could no longer control himself. He put the blunt between his lips and held on to her hips as she bounced up and down. When he couldn't take it anymore, he exploded inside of her. That still didn't stop her. She continued to ride him until she came.

He lifted her off of him, used his towel to wipe them both off, and they laid back on the couch holding each other until they fell asleep.

His girl woke up to the smell of the dinner that she started before they started their session. She had forgotten all about it. She didn't bother to wake him up. She figured that whenever he woke up, she would just warm his food up for him. She hated to see him going through this, and even though they hadn't been together for a long time, she still cared about him. As far as she was concerned, nobody should have to go through what he was going through.

She was with him when his brother was beaten and left in a warehouse to die. She was with him while his brother was found and being nursed back to health and now through his brother's death. She didn't feel very strong at times, and she wasn't sure how much more she could take, but she was doing her best to be there for him and to help him get to the bottom of it.

CHAPTER EIGHT

Jasmine heard a loud noise outside, so she went to see what it was. She was finally feeling better and was gaining a lot of her mobility back without having to rely so much on her prescription medication. She peeked through her blinds to find Anthony rolling up in a big U-Haul moving truck.

What is this man doing? We haven't even packed anything yet, she thought to herself.

She opened up the front door of her apartment, stepped outside on the front porch, and waited for Anthony to come up.

"Anthony, what are you doing? Why did you bring this big ass moving truck over here, and you know we haven't packed anything yet?"

He kissed her on her cheek and walked past her to go into the house.

"Anthony," she called out as she followed him inside.

"Wait a minute, baby. I gotta pee."

Jasmine shook her head and took baby Malcolm to the

couch to sit down. She loved how he was becoming a little bit more alert. He was beginning to keep his eyes open more, and although his vision wasn't clear yet, he would sometimes stare in the direction of her voice. She couldn't wait until he was able to really focus on her. She knew that he could feel her love. Malcolm was always a breath of fresh air for everyone who encountered him.

"That boy is going to be spoiled rotten," Anthony said when he came out of the bathroom.

"Oh well, he's my first child. What do you expect?"

"I expect you to be dong just what you're doing. I have no complaints," he assured her.

"?

"I told you that I was going to break your lease so you can move."

"But nothing is packed."

"It will be."

Just like clockwork, there was a knock on the door. Jasmine walked over to see who it was. When she looked through the peephole she saw her whole crew. Tamika, Jenna, and Candice were all at the door carrying boxes.

Jasmine didn't say anything. She just looked back at Anthony who was standing there with a big country grin on his face. He walked over to Jasmine and took Malcolm from her.

"Malcolm and I are going out for a father/son day while you beautiful ladies get everything packed up… at least what you can. Me, DeAndre, and some other fellas will be here later to load up the truck. Jasmine, can you please get his diaper bag ready while I get him dressed?"

She stood there with her mouth wide open as she watched Anthony carry her son to the other room. She couldn't believe that he just volunteered her to do manual labor on a Saturday. It was only seven o'clock in the morning, and he already had her working.

"I haven't eaten anything yet. Are you guys hungry?" she asked her friends.

"Anthony said that he'd order us something in a little while. He's just anxious for us to get started," Jenna told her.

"I think he's trying to hurry and get you packed and the truck loaded before you can change your mind," Candice joked.

"He doesn't have to worry about that. I already agreed, so it is what it is. It's going to be weird not being here anymore."

"We have had a lot of good times here," Candice chimed in.

"Yeah, and bad ones too."

"Jas, is his bag ready yet?" Anthony yelled out from the other room.

"Here it is, Anthony." She handed him the diaper bag.

"We'll be back soon. You ladies have fun now." After giving Jasmine a kiss on her forehead, he was out of the door.

"Take care of my baby," she told him as he walked away.

Jasmine walked back into the house and turned on her radio. The sounds of Chingy and Pretty Willie came blaring through her speakers. Each girl grabbed a box and started filling it with items throughout the house. Jasmine began packing up her things from her bedroom, Candice took the kitchen, Tamika took the bathroom, and Jenna packed up the living room.

They worked for about four hours straight, just listening to music and engaging in the occasional small talk. At first, the thought of having to pack up and move was very overwhelming for Jasmine, but with all of her girls pitching in to help, it made it go so much more smoothly.

At about noon, Anthony walked in with baby Malcolm sleeping peacefully in his car seat. DeAndre walked in behind him with food in his hands. He walked in carrying five Imo's pizzas, a variety of flavors of Imo's chicken wings, and several two-liter sodas.

"Dang, y'all. I packed all the dishes up already," Candice told them.

"You forgot who you were dealing with, sis. I got you." Anthony held up another bag with styrofoam plates, cups, silverware, and napkins. He had a big smile on his face because he already knew that they were going to forget to leave that stuff out.

"Why did you get so many pizzas?" Jasmine questioned while she was getting Malcolm out of his car seat and into his crib.

"Y'all been working all day. I didn't know how hungry you were. Plus, we grown ass men got grown ass appetites."

"Yes, because I'm shole about to fuck this up," DeAndre said, rubbing his hands together.

Candice cracked a smile but quickly wiped it off of her face before anyone noticed. She didn't want anybody reading anything into it like Jasmine did with their interaction before.

"How much more do you all have left to pack?"

"Not much. We're almost finished."

"So when we finish eating, we can start loading up the truck?"

"Yep."

Anthony was ecstatic that Jasmine had finally agreed to move into his house. He had townhomes, condos, and houses all over St. Louis, but he had one specifically that he thought would be great for her.

Jasmine finished eating first. She got up and threw her trash away so that she could get back to work. She walked into her kitchen and popped a few pain pills just so that she could have the strength to finish packing. Walking around her apartment from room to room, she thought of the day that she first moved in there. She was so excited; she felt like she was free and independent. She knew that she and her girls would have a bunch of movie nights and slumber parties, and for a little while, things did go as planned. When Corey came in the picture, things started to change as it usually did when people got into relationships.

She would sometimes blow her friends off to spend more time with him and not always because she wanted to, but because he started to demand it. He never wanted her to spend time with her friends or family. The family part was easy because she didn't have much family there, but her friends were always there and wanted to spend time with her. As she continued to walk through her apartment, she saw an area on a wall where she had to pay one of the maintenance men that worked at her apartment complex a few dollars on the side to patch up a wall because Corey came home drunk one night and mad for no reason. He pushed the door open with so much force that it put a hole in the wall.

"Hey, girl, you alright?" Candice asked her when she saw her friend walking slowly through the apartment but not packing anything.

"If you need to rest, sit down, and we can finish this."

"I'm good. Just thinking. That's all."

"Come on. Let's get this over with so that we can go and decorate your new home," Candice said with a smile. She wasn't sure what her friend was feeling at the moment, but she just wanted her to be happy.

"Let me talk to you for a minute." Candice felt a tug on her arm and looked to find DeAndre pulling her.

She just stood there and looked at him. She didn't want to be with him alone. He had only kissed her once, and things between them had already gotten awkward. That's what she didn't want to happen. That's why she didn't want to pursue anything with him. Relationships fucked up friendships. She liked the friendship that they already had.

"Go ahead, C. I'll be okay," Jasmine assured her.

Candice followed DeAndre onto the balcony. When she came out, he pulled the blinds closed so that no one inside of the apartment could see them. Candice didn't say anything; she just waited for him to start. He didn't speak right away either. He wanted to get his words together before he said anything. He looked at her and then looked away. He did it one more time.

"DeAndre, will you just tell me whatever it is you want to say. You out here being all dramatic. What's the deal?"

He turned around and looked at her with his eyebrows raised out of shock. He couldn't believe that she had just snapped at him, but he had to admit he kind of liked it.

"We've been in the same room together for an hour, and you haven't acknowledged me once. Hell, you didn't even speak when I came in the door like you usually do."

"Boy, what is your issue for real? I don't owe you anything."

"You right, but I can't get a 'hi, Dre,' or 'what's up, DeAndre' no more?"

"Man, you are really buggin'."

He moved in a little bit closer to her. She immediately stepped back, but he stepped forward again. She couldn't deny the chemistry between them. She wondered why she never felt it before. They had been friends for a long time, and they had hung in the same circle many times, but up until a few days ago, she never thought of him as being attractive or anything.

"Candice, I'm sorry for crossing the line with you the other day. I saw the opportunity, and I took it. I hope you can forgive me for that."

"I told you before, it's cool, man. I forgive you," she said as she took another step back. She was trying to get him out of her personal space. It seemed like the closer he got to her the more her heart rate sped up. She didn't understand it, but she was trying to save herself.

"Good. I hope you can forgive me for this." DeAndre moved in, taking up her personal space again. He held her face in both of his hands and kissed her gently on her lips. This time, she didn't resist. She just went with it. What started as a peck on the lips ended up being a full-on tongue twist. His hands moved from her face to her waist, and she wrapped hers around his neck. DeAndre slowly backed her up against the brick wall with their lips still attached.

"Well, what the fuck do we have here?" Anthony asked

while standing in the doorway, holding his cup in his hand. He gave them a sly grin. He had a feeling that they were feeling each other, but he wasn't sure because DeAndre never said anything about it. It was just a vibe that he was catching.

The sound of his voice startled Candice, and she jumped like she was a sixteen-year-old girl that just got caught with a boy in her room. She didn't even bother to make eye contact with Anthony; she just lowered her head in embarrassment. DeAndre laughed at the expression that Anthony had on his face.

"Aye, man, we were just talking," DeAndre lied, still laughing.

"And then what happened, you just decided to swallow the girl? Let me tell you two something. It is daytime, and you are outside. People can really see you," Anthony joked. Without another word, Anthony went back into the house to give them their privacy. Candice rested her head back against the wall that she was leaning on.

"You didn't resist me," DeAndre whispered in her ear.

"I couldn't," she told him while wiping her mouth.

"So, you're not mad?"

"DeAndre, this right here is freaking me out. I don't know where it all came from, but I do feel something between us. I can't say what because I don't know, and I don't even know if I want it, but it's there. I'm not mad, but I don't know if I want it to keep happening. Let's not mess up what we have, D."

"How do you know that we can't have something better, though?"

"You saying you want to be my man?"

"I'm saying I want to let things flow naturally, Candice. If more comes out of it, good, but I don't want you to keep resisting me. You keep blocking something that has the potential to be great."

"Just give me time." Candice pushed him up off of her so that she could step away. She was on her way into the house when he stopped her.

"I have one more thing to talk to you about."

She stopped in her tracks and rolled her eyes before turning to face him.

"Come on, C. Don't give me attitude. This is serious."

"I'm listening."

"Me and Anthony went over Corey's baby mother's house the other day to throw her a few stacks for covering for you."

Candice's heart dropped down into the pit of her stomach when he said that. Her thoughts instantly went back to that night. She wanted to forget about it so bad, but she knew that it was going to keep coming up. DeAndre could see the worry on her face. Her facial expression went from attitude to terror. He walked closer to her and whispered.

"She swore to keep quiet. She said that the detectives had been to her house a few times to go over her story, but they don't have any leads, of course. They will be contacting us so that we can go to the station and give a formal statement about what happened, but if we can come up with the same story and convince them that it's true, it could be an open shut case."

DeAndre wrapped his arms around Candice. He hugged her to offer moral support. He knew that it was a sensitive subject for her, and every time it was brought up, she got tense. He didn't make any moves on her this time. He wanted to be the friend that she wanted him to be, and at that moment he knew that she needed one. She accepted the hug for all that it was. It felt so good to her to be wrapped in someone's arms, and so be it if it had to be his. She had been stressing about the situation with Corey ever since the night it happened. She didn't want to go to jail. The thought of it frightened her.

She inhaled deeply and held it for a few seconds before exhaling. "Thank you, Dre," she said before releasing his embrace and heading back to the apartment.

"I'm gon' walk with you through this, C. You don't have to face this alone," he told her before she went in. She just turned around and flashed him a smile.

DeAndre stood out on the balcony a little longer so that he could gather his thoughts. He told himself that he had to stop pushing up on Candice. He knew that in order to get the results he wanted from her, he was going to have to stop pushing up on her. He decided that the best thing for them was for him to give her some space.

"Hey, man, the ladies are ready for us to load the truck

up," Anthony said, standing in the doorway again.

DeAndre responded with a nod and just went back into the house and started grabbing boxes.

CHAPTER NINE

Jasmine walked into her new house with her son in her arms. The first thing she noticed was the marble floor in the foyer and the fancy chandelier that hung above her head. The architecture in the entryway was absolutely gorgeous. Her mouth had been opened wide in amazement ever since they pulled up into the driveway. The front lawn was beautiful with even more beautiful flowers that sat in a straight line from the curb to where the walkway began. It was not like she wasn't used to nice things or had not been in big houses. She'd been in a few but not any that she was planning on living in.

"Anthony, this is beautiful, but what am I going to do with all of this space?" She continued to explore the house with her eyes.

"Come on, babe. This is your house now. You can do whatever you want to do with it. Come in. You can't stand in the doorway forever," he joked.

"Here." Jasmine handed Malcolm over to Candice so that she could explore her new home. Everything was so white. It didn't look like he had ever done anything to the house. It had some furniture in it, none that she would have picked out, but it would have to work until she was able to get some more in there.

While Jasmine, Jenna, Tamika, and Candice went their separate ways to look around the house, DeAndre, Anthony, and the guys that Anthony hired to help unload the truck started grabbing boxes. When the girls were packing, they labeled every box for the room of the house they were supposed to go into to make it easier for the guys.

Jasmine made her way to the master bedroom, which had a bathroom attached. It was one of the most beautiful rooms she'd ever seen. At least the layout of it was. There weren't many decorations in there either. She was just in awe of everything she saw.

"Hey, babe, this house is so beautiful. Why haven't you decorated it, though?" Jasmine asked when Anthony walked in to drop off a box of her things.

"I never lived in it, so I didn't need to decorate it."

"So you just bought this house?"

"Nope. It's a house that I already had. I just never lived in it."

"So how many houses do you have?"

"I have a few, but this one is yours, so enjoy it."

Anthony was always so secretive about how he made his money. That was always something that concerned her because she never wanted to get caught up in no mess about anything illegal. When she first found the bag full of money in her home, she thought that it was drug money, but he assured her that it wasn't, and she just went with it. She trusted him, and he always promised to eventually tell her how he made his money. He told her that it was nothing bad or anything to worry about, just something that he didn't talk about much.

She blew it off for the moment because she wanted to go and see the rest of the house, but she made a mental note to find out about it later. Before she could leave out of the master bedroom, Jenna came in.

"Girl, have you seen the kitchen yet?"

"I haven't made it that far. Come on, show me where it is."

Excitedly, Jenna held on to Jasmine's arm and led the way to the kitchen. Jasmine loved the details that adorned the room from the double ovens, the floors, backsplash design, granite countertops, and the bay window with a seating area. Overall, the house was beautiful to her. It wasn't the best house, but it was the best house for her and her family. Besides, it was a big step up from where she was coming from.

Her favorite part of the house was the inground swimming pool that sat in her new backyard, as well as the deck area to entertain her guests, and the patio for Anthony to show off his skills on the grill. There was more than enough room out there for Malcolm to play once he got big enough. The rest of the house was nice, but when she went to look in the back, she just felt like that was her spot. If anyone was ever looking for her, she knew that they'd find her there.

"I think he's ready to eat, mama. He's been fussing on and off for awhile now. Me rocking him is no longer working," Candice said, handing her godson back to his mommy.

Jasmine had become a breastfeeding pro by then. She didn't care where she was or who was there, she popped that boob out and fed her baby. While he ate, she sat on the deck and daydreamed about what all of it meant. She had been given this big beautiful house, she finally had the man of her dreams, and materialistically there was nothing she wanted. She had everything she needed. Now, she had to figure out what she was going to do with it all.

"Hey, babe, we are done unloading the truck. All of the boxes should be where they are supposed to go," Anthony said, peeking his head outside.

As soon as Jasmine turned around to acknowledge him, Tamika and Jenna came walking past him. They both took a seat at the table that she and Candice were sitting at.

"So how do you like your new spot?" Tamika asked. She had her issues with Jasmine and the other girls sometimes, but she still genuinely had a love for all of them. They had a friendship that turned into a sisterhood, and sisters fought, right?

"I think it is gorgeous. Anthony said that the house was in Ladue, and I already knew that Ladue was full of really nice houses, but I didn't expect it to be like this. This house is modern, but it has its country accents to it," Jasmine replied.

"I can't wait to get you settled in here so that we can have our sleepovers like we used to have," Jenna said.

"Girl, please. We don't even need a girl's night. I'm sleeping over anyway just because. The house is so damn big, they won't even know I'm here," Candice said.

Her comment made everybody laugh. Jasmine could picture herself waking up in the morning to find Candice sleeping somewhere in the house. Candice didn't care. She'd sleep on the floor, the bed, couch, or chair. That's just the way she was. She took her role as sister seriously. They weren't blood sisters, but she sure did act like it.

"It's almost time to start planning this wedding," Jenna stated.

Jasmine's face lit up thinking about her wedding. She always got butterflies in her stomach when she thought about walking down the aisle and meeting her best friend at the end. With all of the drama and chaos going on in her life, she hadn't had much time to think about her wedding.

But with her new house and her new beginning, she knew that it was time.

Anthony and the guys went back to the apartment to clean up and turn in Jasmine's keys. The girls stayed behind and started unpacking boxes. The first thing they did was set up Jasmine and Anthony's room so that Jasmine and Malcolm could finally lay down and get some rest. They had been up all day, and even though she denied needing rest, they knew she needed it.

She had it easy, though. She sat down in a chair in the corner of her room and told everybody where she wanted her things, and they made sure it was placed just like she instructed. When they were done, she and the baby laid down while the girls tackled other rooms of the house. She wasn't there to tell them where to put things, so they just had to wing it until she could get up and tell them or do the rearranging herself.

When Jasmine finally woke up, she sat up on her bed and looked around her new bedroom. She was still in awe of everything that her new home had to offer. She didn't mind that the walls were bare or that a lot of things were undecorated because she knew that she wouldn't have to do much to spruce it up like she wanted. Everything would be new and fresh. She had too many limitations to what she could do in her apartment since it was rented. The apartment managers wouldn't let her express herself or her creativity. She was happy to finally have her own stuff, and there wasn't anybody that could tell her what she could and couldn't do.

She looked over to where her prince was still sleeping, and she carried him over to his crib that sat next to her bed. She had the girls set it up in her room instead of in his because she wasn't ready to be apart from him yet. She was still a little spooked about how Corey was able to come into her apartment and take him from right up under her while she slept, so him being all the way in another room in such a big house was out of the question.

She placed one part of his baby monitor inside of his crib and tucked the other one away in her pocket. She headed down the long hallway that led to her spiral staircase. As she walked downstairs she began to notice some things that she didn't see earlier. She was just taking it all in.

"There you are," she sang when she saw all of her friends spread all over the kitchen floor eating. She was looking around at what each person had, being nosy.

"Don't think you about to put yo' hands in my food. You have food right over there," Candice told her while pointing at a Panda Express bag on the counter. Jasmine smiled because she liked that her friends knew what she liked. She was able to take a nap and wake up to a delicious meal without having to deal with the stress of trying to decide what to eat.

"You guys have been working all day. If you want to leave after you eat, I'll be fine."

"I'll leave when Anthony gets back. I just don't feel comfortable leaving you alone with the baby just yet. You might need help with something, and no one will be here to help you," Jenna expressed her concern.

"I'll be fine. You guys can go," Jasmine protested.

"Are you trying to get rid of us?" Candice asked.

"No, I just know that you all may have something else to do."

After all of the debating back and forth about whether they should stay or go, everybody decided to stay. When they finished eating dinner, they all went into the den and turned on a movie. Everybody found their own spot on the floor and camped out with a blanket. Before they got too comfortable, Tamika ran upstairs to get Malcolm and extra diapers and wipes so that they wouldn't have to interrupt the movie to get him if he cried.

The girls spent the next hour and a half taking turns reciting the lines from *The Player's Club*. It felt good to everyone to be in the each other's company, in good spirits, and getting along despite all that was happening to and around them. Everybody was able to put on a smile, even though they were dealing with their own set of issues.

Anthony put his key in the front door of the house and let himself in. DeAndre trailed behind him. The other guys that Anthony paid to help them earlier that day had already gone their own way. He walked through the house and straight into the kitchen, calling Jasmine but never got an answer.

"Damn, they ate good," Anthony said, looking at all of

the empty containers of Panda Express on the kitchen counters.

He continued to call her name as he walked through the house, but he still never got a response.

"Look here, dog," DeAndre told him, waving him to the room that sat toward the back of the house. When Anthony went to see what he was talking about, he laughed.

"Looks like the ultimate girl's night," he said.

All of the girls fell asleep right where they were when the movie started. Malcolm was on his own little pallet on the floor next to his mom. Anthony decided not to wake them. He turned the television off and left them there to rest.

"I guess I'll catch up with y'all later then," DeAndre told him. They gave each other a bro hug, and he headed out to his car.

Anthony went and cleaned up the mess the girls left in the kitchen and locked up the house. It was a task since there were so many doors and windows that had to be checked, but it was worth it to him to know that his family was safe. When he was done, he went into his man cave and checked his surveillance cameras. He wanted to make sure that all of his cameras were set and facing the way that he wanted. Also, he wanted to run them back over the last few hours to make sure that nothing suspicious had happened while he was gone. He didn't bother to tell Jasmine that the house was covered in cameras because he knew that it would bother her. Most of them were focused on the perimeter of the house anyway and not inside so that she wouldn't feel like her privacy was being compromised.

When he was done with everything, he went upstairs to his room, took a shower, and fell asleep alone.

CHAPTER TEN

It was a new day, and it was beautiful outside. The sun was shining bright, there was a light breeze, and birds were chirping. Jasmine was bouncing through the house excited that Anthony had agreed to take her to pick out some new furniture. She had already been window shopping online and trying her hardest not to order anything because she was waiting for this day.

When she got herself and Malcolm ready for their day out, they sat out on the back patio to wait for Anthony to finish getting ready. She had to be excited because he was usually the one waiting for her to get ready but not today.

"Hey, Jas, where you at?" She heard Anthony calling for her through the house so she just went back in. She didn't want to wake Malcolm up by yelling back to him. She stopped in the kitchen to get herself a glass of water as he made his way to her.

"Hey, baby. You ready?" He asked, walking up behind her and kissing her on her neck.

"I figured you'd find me. Yes, I'm ready. My purse and

Malcolm's diaper bag are sitting on the chair at the front door."

Anthony took the baby from her to put him in his car seat. He liked to show off his skills. He had gotten much better than the day at the hospital when he put Malcolm in his car seat the wrong way. Jasmine didn't mind. She just smiled at him and let him bask in the happiness about his new accomplishments. She sat down on the passenger side of Anthony's car and adjusted the seat while the baby was being secured in his spot in the back of the car.

"You look good, girl," Anthony told Jasmine as she applied lipstick and touched up the makeup on her cheeks.

"Thanks, boo."

When she finished looking herself over, she sat back in her seat and crossed her legs. She was ready for her day. She felt like she hadn't really been out of the house much since the baby was born.

She must really be recovered from her C-Section, Anthony thought to himself as he pushed Malcolm in his stroller a few feet behind Jasmine. She was all over the place. She had them in Lowe's, Home Depot, Ikea, Target, and J.C. Penney trying to find all of the right things for their new home. Everything in each room had to coordinate with the right colors and designs, and all of the décor and designs had to flow from room to room throughout the house. Jasmine was giving a new meaning to shopping 'til you drop. He tried to convince her to go home and finish her shopping online, but she said that she'd get all that she could at the store, and whatever she forgot, she'd get online. They had bags in each hand, tucked in the bottom of the stroller, and still had a shit load of things that had to be delivered to the house. When Anthony told her that the new house was a canvas waiting for her finishing touches, she took that to heart. He gave her a credit card but wouldn't tell her the limit on it. He just told her to get whatever she wanted.

"I didn't think you were going to ever stop," Anthony said as he looked over his menu, happy to finally be able to sit down.

"Well, I knew we had to eat something. Plus, the baby has to eat," she replied.

Sitting in 54th Grill and Bar waiting for the waitress to

135

come and take their drink orders, Jasmine's mind wandered back to where they had their first date. That whole date was full of drama and chaos. She smiled when she thought of the way she reacted when she was met with a waitress that was off the chain. She expressed feelings that she didn't even realize she had. That was the day that Anthony poured his heart out to her, and even then, she didn't believe him. Back then, she wouldn't have even thought about being where she was in her life at that moment.

"What are you smiling so hard about?" Anthony asked her.

"I was just thinking about us. I'm happy that we were finally able to get it together."

"For awhile, I didn't think that you would come around. You were so stuck on Corey that you wouldn't even look in my direction."

"I thought that I was doing the right thing. I didn't want to leave a long relationship because something new came along."

"Something new? I was here before he was. I was gone

for a minute, but I came back as usual."

"A minute my ass. You were gone for a few years. I'm glad you came back around, though. I'm glad that my son will have an excellent role model in his life. We both need you."

Anthony didn't say anything else. He held on to Jasmine's hands across the table and lifted them one by one so that he could plant a kiss on each one.

"Thanks for everything, Anthony. I'm not just talking about the house or anything else that you have provided. Thank you for being here," Jasmine said sincerely.

Once again, Anthony didn't say anything. All of sudden, the cat had his tongue, and he couldn't verbally express his feelings. Every time he thought about how he really felt for Jasmine, it did something to him that he couldn't really explain. He could say that he loved her, and he told her that all of the time, but the love that he had for her sometimes overwhelmed him. Over the years, Anthony had his fair share of women, but none of them made him feel like Jasmine did.

The waitress came over to take their drink orders. They

ordered their food too. Jasmine peeped that he didn't respond to her thank you, but she blew it off. She didn't want to read too much into it and make something out of nothing.

"I'll be right back. I want to change Malcolm and feed him before our food comes," Jasmine announced. She picked the baby up and grabbed his diaper bag. Anthony stood up to help her. When she was out of sight, he took his cell phone out of his pocket to check his messages. He heard his phone beep awhile ago, but he didn't like being on his phone when he was spending quality time with Jasmine. He thought it was only polite to give her his undivided attention when they were together.

Dre: Aye bro, me and Candice are going to the police department today to give them the formal statements they asked for. We were supposed to go sooner but I just wanted to make sure she had her head in the game before we went. I just wanted to keep you up on what's going on in case some bullshit went down. Somebody needed to know where we were.

He also received some messages from some of the guys

that he does business with, but he figured he'd get back with them later.

Meanwhile, Jasmine had changed Malcolm's diaper and pulled out his blanket and sling so that she could prepare to breastfeed him. She thought that it was so tacky breastfeed a baby at the table in the middle of a public dining room, but she had no choice. There was nowhere else for her to do it. There were times that she sat in the bathroom to feed him, but she didn't feel like she should have to do that, so she never did it again. She placed him in his sling and covered him up so that no one else had to see what was going on and went back out to her table.

She was relieved that her salad had made it to the table by the time she got back. She was starving, and since baby was eating she knew that she would be able to eat in peace.

"Is everything okay?" she asked Anthony when she saw him tuck his cell phone away when she came out of the bathroom.

"Everything is fine. I got a message from Dre, telling me that he and Candice were going to the police department to give their statements of what happened."

"Aw man. I wonder why she didn't tell me," she expressed

"I don't know, but everything should be fine. I'm sure DeAndre has everything under control."

They sat quietly for a minute to take a few bites of their food. The waitress had come back to make sure that everything was okay.

"When we are done eating, I'm going to drop you and Malcolm off at home, and I have to go take care of some business. It shouldn't take me long, though," Anthony stated in between sips of his drink.

"Anthony, we've had such a great day together. Can you please just take the day off so we can continue our night together?" she pleaded.

"I just have some things that I need to check on. I won't be long. I promise."

Jasmine figured it would be pointless to continue going back and forth with him. He was determined to do what he wanted to do, and he always wanted to work. If she didn't know any better she would have thought that, he was seeing another woman because he was always "working."

The only thing that made her believe that he wasn't being foul was the fact that he came home every night, he always had money, and that nothing or no one ever gave her a reason to doubt him. If his money came up short, he stayed out all night, or had some women calling her or beating his door down then yeah, she would be questioning it. She just figured he was a hard-working man that did what he had to do to provide for her and her son.

"Well, I'm a little tired anyway. I guess I'll go home, take a shower, and lay down to rest."

She knew she had pushed her body to the limit, but she would have rather been laying up with him all night.

"Thanks for understanding, Jas,' he said with a smile.

The two of them enjoyed their food over small talk. Anthony had another round of drinks before heading home. They wound down to the sounds of Jill Scott on their way back to their house. Jasmine laid her seat back and relaxed as Anthony cruised through the city's streets. He rested his left hand on the steering wheel and his right hand on her thigh.

As soon as they got in the house, Jasmine didn't waste

any time getting undressed. From the front door, up the stairs, and into her bedroom she was snatching off pieces of clothing. She had worn herself out and was ready for bed.

"I'll be right back," Anthony told her before leaving out of the bedroom. He headed down to the room where all of his surveillance cameras were set up. He wanted to look at the footage before he left to go on his business run. He didn't expect anything to happen, but he knew that he couldn't be too sure with all of the things that had been happening lately. Jasmine had just moved into that house, and nobody was supposed to know that she was there except her close friends. His number one goal was to keep her and their baby safe.

When he was satisfied with the lack of activity around his property, he closed the room back up and went back to his bedroom to kiss Jasmine goodnight. By the time he got to her, the baby was sound asleep in his crib, and she was in the shower. He peeked his head in and was pushed back by all of the heat and steam coming out the bathroom.

"Got damn, baby. It's hot in there. I wanted to kiss you

goodnight, but I can't even breathe in there," Anthony told her, trying to preserve his breath.

"So you mean to tell me you couldn't walk through steam to get to me. Am I not that important to you?" she asked.

"You already know that I'd do anything for you. Don't play with me," he told her.

"Prove it then," she challenged.

Anthony shook his head because he knew that she was just messing with him, but he had to back up what he said, so he went in. He walked through the hot, steamy bathroom to get to his fiancée.

"Why you always testing me, girl?" he asked her when he pulled the shower curtain back to get the kiss he originally wanted.

"Just kiss me," Jasmine told him, standing there with a big smile on her face.

Anthony did as he was told and leaned in to kiss Jasmine. She reciprocated and kissed him passionately. She kept her tongue moving to keep him distracted while she lowered her hand to get a handful of his dick which, to her surprise, was already hard. He quickly pulled away from her.

"Come on, Jay, you know I gotta go, and you getting my clothes all wet," he fussed.

"Oh, I forgot you were leaving," she lied.

"You didn't forget," he told her.

"You mad?" she teased.

"Naw, I ain't mad. I just don't want to have to change clothes."

Jasmine turned the water off in the shower and grabbed her towel off the towel rack. She wrapped it around her and dried her feet off on the rug next to the bathtub. She brushed past Anthony, who was standing there trying to fix his clothes.

When he went back out into the bedroom he saw Jasmine laying on the bed with her towel underneath her. The sight of the water running down her naked body turned him on.

"Turn over," he told her.

She didn't ask any questions. Instead, she just did as she was told. She turned over and rested on her stomach.

Anthony reached to the center of the bed and gently pulled her down toward him. He unfastened the belt on his pants, released the button and let them fall to the floor. He slid his boxers down then bent over to lift her up. She put a dip in her back, and he spread her legs. When she was positioned just the way wanted her, he penetrated her effortlessly. She moaned immediately. They had done it several times since Malcolm was born, but this is the first time that she felt comfortable doing it in this way, and this was her favorite position.

Her pussy was so tight, she felt like a virgin. That in itself turned both of them on. He loved the way she used her muscles to squeeze his dick as he stroked.

"Uh un, baby, don't run from it. This is what you wanted, right?" he asked her when he felt her inching away from him.

The more she resisted, the harder he pounded her.

"Where are you going? Throw it back, Jay," he continued his shit talking.

"Whose pussy is this?" he asked through clenched teeth.

"Yours," she moaned.

"Whose?"

"Your's, baby. It's yours," she told him.

Jasmine threw her ass back on Anthony, causing his dick to go deeper. She matched his pace, and every time she threw it back, it brought him closer to his climax.

Jasmine clenched the sheets and put her head on the pillow in front of her.

"I'm about to cum, Ant!" she yelled out, and that did it for him.

He exploded inside of her with that last stroke. He tried to keep stroking to get a second one off, but he didn't have it in him. He went into their bathroom and got a washcloth with warm water on it and wiped her off. When he was done, she crawled up on the bed and got underneath the covers. He went back into the bathroom and cleaned himself up. He wanted to go to the meeting that he had already planned on going to, but when he saw Jasmine resting peacefully, he couldn't fight his urge to join her. He turned the bathroom lights off and climbed into the bed and cuddled up behind her. They both fell asleep instantly.

CHAPTER ELEVEN

Jasmine woke up the next morning to her cell phone ringing. She was so tired, it felt like she had a hangover. She picked it up only to see that she had three missed calls. They were all from Candice. After several minutes of contemplating in her head if she should call her back right now or not, she decided to since Anthony had already gotten out of the bed. She didn't have a reason to stay in it.

After washing her face and brushing her teeth, she dialed Candice's phone number back by pushing the speed dial button on the phone.

"Girl it must be something really important for you to be blowing my phone up like you have been," Jasmine told her.

"It is. DeAndre asked me out. Like on a real date. What am I supposed to tell him?" Candice asked, sounding like a schoolgirl that was just asked out by the most popular guy in school.

"Well, do you want to go on a date with him?"

"No. I don't think so."

"That doesn't even make sense, Candice. You two have hung out countless times, so what is the big deal?"

"The big deal is that he isn't trying to hang out. He wants it to be a real one on one date. Every time I talk to him, he is on some sweet, romantic type shit."

"Okay and? You like him, right?" Jasmine asked, cutting her off.

"Yeah, I guess."

"Then go on a date with him, child. We got other things to worry about, so I need y'all to get this show on the road," Jasmine demanded.

"What other stuff do we have to worry about?"

"Wedding planning," Jasmine sang into the phone.

"Tamika was right. It is always about Princess Jasmine," Candice joked.

"Don't even start with me about that girl. She be tripping hard."

"Well, check this out. Since you scared to go on a date with Dre, why don't everybody come over here and we have a lil' cookout type thing, and y'all can chill here? Just know if y'all come over here, we gon' be all up in yo' business."

"That's cool. When?"

"Tomorrow's Saturday. Let's do it then," Jasmine suggested.

"Cool."

"Alright. I'll see you tomorrow at about one o'clock," Jasmine confirmed.

Jasmine looked over at Malcolm's bed and saw that he wasn't in there. She knew he had to be somewhere in the house with Anthony. She slipped on her house shoes, tied her satin robe around her waist, and headed out of the bedroom to go look for them.

She peeked into every room as she made her way down the hall. When she couldn't find them upstairs, she skipped down the stairs of her spiral staircase and checked the kitchen and the family room. Still nothing. She finally made it to the lower level of the house. She started to hear the joyful noises coming from her baby, so she followed his voice. When she finally found them, they were in Anthony's man cave. First, she peeked her head in before going all the way in. Anthony was holding Malcolm on his leg facing him, holding both of his hands and bouncing him. Malcolm kept giggling and laughing. Hearing his laugh made her laugh a little. She loved seeing Anthony play with Malcolm. He really did treat him like he was his biological child.

"Hey, baby," Anthony said when he saw Jasmine standing in the doorway.

"What's up? What's all of this stuff?" she asked, speaking of the cameras.

"It's just my top-notch security system," he bragged.

"So are all the cameras for outside, or do you have any inside the house too?"

"Both. You don't have anything to worry about though. I ain't spying on you," he teased.

"I sure hope not. There's no telling what you might see if you start spying on me."

Anthony looked at her with a raised eyebrow. "Is that so? A peep show wouldn't be a bad surprise," he told her.

"You wish."

"Off the subject," she continued with the real reason that she went looking for Anthony in the first place. "I think we should have a cookout here tomorrow afternoon."

"I'm cool with that. Who's coming?"

"The usual. Nothing fancy. I might invite a few more people. For the most part, it'll just be the usual."

"You know I don't care who you invite, but just keep in mind the reason you moved out here in the first place."

"Babe, everything will be fine. I wouldn't invite anyone to our home that I thought would bring us trouble or unnecessary drama."

"Is there anything you need from me for this gathering?"

"Some money would be nice," she told him with a smile.

"I should have known."

Anthony dug into his wallet and handed his credit card over to Jasmine. She excitedly took it from him and ran upstairs to shower and get herself together. After her shower, she dressed, unwrapped her hair, applied a little bit of makeup, grabbed her purse, and left. She loved to entertain, so every time she got the chance to, she went all out. She told herself that she wasn't going to go overboard, but when she went into the stores, she couldn't help herself. She bought everything from serving dishes, eating dishes, accessories, and a whole new grill. She knew that Anthony was going to think she lost her mind, but she didn't care.

When she was confident that she had gotten all that she needed, she headed home. She was excited to show Anthony what she got. She smiled as she whipped her truck through traffic, listening to Mary J. Blige's *What's the 411* album. The thought of her life finally coming together brought her so much joy, even the thought of her two best friends finding something in each other. She couldn't call it love yet, but she knew that it was something.

Pulling into her driveway, she took in the scenery. She felt blessed to be able to live where she was. She fought Anthony about moving, but it proved to be a great decision. She had tried her hand at gardening, and she couldn't wait to see her flowers bloom. The spring was coming, and she could smell it in the air.

Jasmine unloaded her truck of all of her shopping bags.

She couldn't even get all the way to the front door before the front door flew open.

"Hey, baby. Did you enjoy yourself?" Anthony asked her.

"That can't be a serious question. You know I enjoy myself every time I'm shopping."

"Well, it sure does look like you didn't forget anything," he told her.

"I tried not to," she joked.

"Who is that?" Anthony asked, referring to the big delivery truck pulling up in his driveway behind Jasmine's tuck.

Jasmine turned around to see the Lowe's truck pulling up.

"Oh good. They were fast."

Anthony looked at her in confusion. "What did you order that you needed it to be delivered?" he asked.

"I bought a grill," she responded nonchalantly.

"Jay, we already have a grill."

"I know, but that was my old grill from the old apartment. I wanted something new to start new memories.

If that makes sense."

He wasn't too thrilled with her buying a new grill, but he couldn't argue with her logic.

"Where do you want us to sit this?" the passenger of the delivery truck asked.

"Give me a second. I'll open up the side gate for you."

The two men went to the back of the truck and retrieved the barbecue grill with a dolly. By the time they got it and made it to the side of the house, Jasmine had already had the gate open.

"You can go ahead and put it right over there," Jasmine pointed in the direction that she wanted them to put it.

She walked out of the side gate with them and tipped them both fifty dollars each. "Thank you guys so much," she said.

They wished her well and went on their way.

Jasmine went back to the front of the house to get the rest of her bags that she left on the porch when she saw the delivery truck pull up, and they were already gone.

"I left your bags in the family room," Anthony yelled when he heard her come through the door.

She grabbed her bags and took them all into the kitchen where Anthony was with a sleeping Malcolm.

"Hey, babe, you want to see what I got?" Jasmine asked excitedly.

She didn't even wait for him to respond. She started pulling her purchased items out of the bags while Anthony watched.

"What's wrong, Anthony? You don't seem happy."

"I'm fine, I just don't understand why you bought stuff that we already had. Every time we have a gathering, you always buy new stuff, but we already have it."

"Most of the things we already have, but I just got it in a different color or pattern. You know, something to switch as the season's change to freshen up the scenery a little bit." Jasmine tried to get him to understand where she was coming from.

"Hey, whatever you like is fine with me," he told her.

"I have a few phone calls to make. I'll be in the office," Anthony told her before he kissed her forehead and walked out of the kitchen.

Jasmine sat down at the table and tried to figure out

what had just happened. She couldn't figure out if Anthony was mad at the fact that she bought more stuff, if he was mad that she bought a new grill, or what he was mad at. She didn't understand, but she could tell that something wasn't right with him. She tried to put it in the back of her mind so that she could take her newly bought items out and put them away before Malcolm woke up. When she was done, she grabbed Malcolm's baby monitor, poured herself a glass of wine, and sat out on her deck in the backyard.

She loved it out there. It was so peaceful, and she was able to be one with her thoughts. Her day had gone so good before she came back home, and she was determined to not let anyone, even Anthony, ruin it. As the day began to come to an end and the sun started to set, she stared up at the sky as it changed colors. She sipped her wine and enjoyed the moment of peace before she had to go back and resume her motherly duties.

CHAPTER TWELVE

Anthony woke up to Jasmine singing in the shower. She was feeling good. After about three glasses of wine and play time with her son, she had gotten completely over her issue with Anthony. She didn't know what he was tripping off of the day before, and he didn't bother to tell her, so she just let it go. They had never had any real arguments. Their communication always seemed to be good, so she didn't want to start something with him when it was probably nothing in the first place.

He went into the bathroom where she was to pee, brush his teeth, and wash his face. Just like before, he was hit in the face with a cloud of steam, but this time, he didn't complain. He just dealt with it.

Jasmine cringed at the sound of Anthony's pee hitting the water. She didn't understand why he had to come into the bathroom where she was. There were other bathrooms in the house. She wanted to say something to him, but she knew that it would end in an argument. She had been feeling so on edge lately, and she didn't know why. Every little thing seemed to piss her off, so she had to constantly check herself so that she wouldn't snap on people.

"Good morning, Jas," Anthony said, noticing that her once boisterous singing turned into a soft hum.

"Hey," she dryly responded.

"What time is this gathering supposed to take place today?" he asked her.

"Twelve, but you guys are going to have to put the new grill together before then unless you just want to wait until everybody gets here. I just don't know how long it's going to take you."

Anthony rolled his eyes at the thought of having to put that grill together. "Yeah, that's right. I forgot all about having to do that."

Just as he was about to ask her another question, he heard Malcolm crying. He washed his hands and eased out of the bathroom.

"Hey, lil' man," Anthony said as he lifted Malcolm up out of his crib.

Immediately, Anthony was greeted with a smile. Anthony didn't know what it was that makes the baby smile and laugh as soon as he saw him, but whatever it was, he loved it. He laid him on the bed to change his diaper. The whole time, they talked and laughed. Anthony enjoyed daddy duties. After being with Jasmine throughout her pregnancy and being with Malcolm ever since he was born, he didn't understand how men could leave and walk out on their children. Being with Malcolm was one of the best things in his life right now. It was hard work sometimes, but it was never hard enough to make him want to leave.

"Is he okay?" Jasmine asked, walking out of the bathroom towel drying her hair.

"He's fine. We were just having a father-son talk. I had to give him the rundown on you women and how you treat us men."

"Aw yeah? Well, you better be telling him the truth."

"I will always tell him the truth," Anthony said while giving baby Malcolm a wink.

"Do you have any idea what kind of food you are serving at this cookout?" he asked her, finishing up the baby's diaper change.

"A few ribs, chicken wings, steaks, hotdogs, and

burgers on the grill with baked beans, potato salad, green beans, creamed eggs, corn on the cob, and a strawberry cheesecake."

"Damn, are you having all of that catered? I know you ain't about to be in the kitchen all day for me, you, Dre, and your girls. That's a whole lot of food."

"Oh, I forgot mac and cheese too. I'm not cooking all of that, and I'm not having it catered. You guys are going to be cooking the meat, and me and the girls are going to cook the sides, but nobody is going to be cooking everything, and I told you that I was inviting a few more people, so it won't be just us."

"As long as you have a plan. I'll go downstairs and get started on assembling this grill."

"I hope this doesn't take a long time," he mumbled to himself. He left the baby on their bed so that Jasmine could get him whenever she was done getting herself together and headed downstairs.

Anthony slid his patio door open and shook his head at the sight of the box that the grill was in. There was nothing in the world that he wouldn't do for Jasmine, but he just didn't feel like doing any manual labor. He figured he'd just do it and get it over with. He thought about calling DeAndre to have him come through and help him assemble the thing but decided against it. He used his phone to turn on some music to help him get motivated. He got the box, cut it open, and took everything out of it. He found the directions and laid them to the side. He didn't plan on using them. He heard Jasmine walking through the house, headed in his direction rapping.

"I ain't a killer, but don't push me. Revenge is like the sweetest joy next to gettin' pussy. Picture paragraphs unloaded wise words bein' quoted. Peeped the weakness in the rap game and sewed it. Bow down, pray to God, hoping that he's listenin'. Seein' niggaz comin' for me, to my diamonds when they glistenin'."

Anthony laughed when she came out on the patio where he was. "Girl, you don't know nothing about this song."

"Boy, you trippin'. This used to be my jam," she said, still bobbing her head to the music. "Me and Malcolm are about to run to the store to pick up some of the ingredients that I'll need to cook with. We'll be back shortly. Have fun with your project." She bobbed her head back through the house still rapping.

"They got an APB out on my thug family since Outlawz run these streets like these scandalous freaks. Our enemies die now, walk around half-dead, head down, K-blasted off of Hennessy, and Thai chronic mixed in. Now, I'm twisted, blistered, and high. Visions of me thug-livin' gettin' me by, forever live, and I multiply. Survived by thugs when I die. They won't cry unless they comin' with slugs."

"Boy yo' daddy trippin. He just don't know. Pac is my boy. I know all of his music," Jasmine told Malcolm. She put him in his car seat, grabbed his diaper bag, and was on her way. She made sure to make a list before she left because she knew that she would forget something, and she didn't want to have to go back to the store once she got home. The store was packed when she got there. It was no way she was going to be able to get in and out like she thought she would. She couldn't believe how many people were there. It was people grocery shopping like

Thanksgiving was a day away.

She took her time cruising up and down the aisles, trying to kill time, and let some of the other shoppers get through the lines so that she wouldn't have to wait in such a long line, but that plan wasn't a good one because the people just kept on coming. She just grabbed everything that was on her list and got in line. Since the line was moving slowly, she used her phone as a distraction. She scrolled through some of her social media pages while she waited. When the line started to move a little more, she looked up and started looking around. That's when she thought she'd saw a ghost. She looked up and saw a face that looked just like Corey's. Kerry was standing near the entrance of the store. To see him shook her. She wanted to leave her basket full of food right where she stood and leave, but in order to do that, she would have to walk past him, so she figured she was better off in that line where she was surrounded by other people. As far as she knew, he hadn't seen her, and she wanted to keep it that way.

Jasmine looked down at her son, who was sitting in the front of the shopping cart snuggled in his car seat. She had to think about his safety and hers, and she didn't want to make a scene. She had no idea how his thought process was about the loss of his brother, and she didn't know if he thought she was the person that killed him. Jasmine and Kerry used to be cool, but things had changed. She just put her head back down and swooped her hair to the side of her face so that she wouldn't be seen.

She hoped that the line would move slowly so that it'd give him enough time to do whatever he was doing and leave before it was time for her to leave the store. She didn't want to cross paths with him. When she realized that she was shaking, she tried to regain her composure. She didn't want to make it obvious to the people around her that there was a problem.

What the hell is he doing all the way over here anyway? she thought to herself. She knew that he didn't live in her neck of the woods, so as far as she was concerned, he shouldn't have been there. There were only two people in front of her, and she hoped that they took their time. He was still at the door, and since she had been looking down, she didn't notice if he had spotted her or not. Malcolm started fussing a little bit, and she hurried to push the grocery cart back and forth in an attempt to calm him down before people started to pay attention to him.

"Oh, he's so precious," the older lady behind her stated.

Jasmine looked at the lady with slanted eyes. She wanted to tell the old lady to back the hell off because she was trying to to be discreet, but she responded anyway. "Thank you," she managed to say in a low tone of voice.

Finally, it was Jasmine's turn at the register, and when she pushed her cart up to the register, she noticed that Kerry was no longer standing at the front of the store. She wondered where he went in just that little time. That short moment that the little old lady said something to her, she lost track of him. Her nerves began to set in. At that moment, all she wanted was to be at home with Anthony. She didn't know what to expect when she left the store. Crazy thoughts started running through her head. *Is he going to kidnap me like we did his brother? Is he going to run me and my baby over with his car? Is he going to whoop my ass, follow me home, or what? What exactly is*

165

his plan? Her mind was racing a million miles a minute.

After the cashier bagged all of their groceries and put them inside of her cart for her, it was time for her to leave. She walked quickly to her car, peeking around corners and looking in between other cars that were parked in the parking lot. She looked at the people that were driving past her. When she made it her car, she immediately snapped Malcolm's car seat into the base and messily threw all of her bags into the trunk of her car. She didn't even bother putting the cart into the designated area for the carts to go into the parking lot. She just left it sitting in the parking spot where her car was.

Normally, Jasmine would have turned on some music and would have been jamming all the way home. She couldn't even focus long enough to think about music. Her main focus was to get out of that parking lot and get back home to her fiancé. She thought about all of those cameras she saw in Anthony's room in the basement. She was happy that they were there so that she could see if she had been followed back to her house. She couldn't remember the last time she felt so scared.

She pulled into her driveway at full speed. She grabbed her baby out of the back seat of her car and didn't even bother to get the bags out of the trunk. Anthony heard her fumbling with her keys at the door and opened it up for her.

"Jasmine, what's wrong with you?" he asked her, seeing that she was clearly shaken by something.

"I saw Kerry at the grocery store, and it freaked me the hell out. I couldn't get out of that damn store fast enough," she told him.

"Did he say anything to you?"

"No. I don't even know if he saw me. I was standing in the checkout line when I saw him standing at the front door. He was there for awhile, but I don't know if he noticed me or not."

"If you don't know if he even saw you, why are you so shaken?"

"Because of what happened to his brother. I don't know what he's thinking right now. What if he thinks I did it or had something to do with it? He knew that me and his brother weren't on good terms, and what if he helped his brother kidnap Malcolm? When Corey left my apartment the night that he took him, he rode away in your car, but he wasn't the one driving. He got into the passenger's seat. Kerry could have been the one driving the car. Seeing him just scared me. That's all."

"You're alright, baby. I'm sorry you had to go through that. I'm glad you're back home safe," Anthony told her as he held her in his arms. He squeezed her tight and kissed the top of her head. He looked up to the sky for guidance. Kerry didn't bother Jasmine or his son this time, but he didn't want him to become a problem. He hoped that it was just a coincidence that he and Jasmine were in the same place at the same time.

"Jay, baby, go take Malcolm and sit down. I'll get the bags out of the car," he told her.

Jasmine did as she was told, still a little agitated. She tried to calm herself so that she could enjoy the rest of the day that she had planned. She hated that she let him get to her like that, and she wasn't even sure if he was there because of her. Jasmine had never been a scary person, but she was just feeling vulnerable. She had gone through too much.

CHAPTER THIRTEEN

Candice walked up to Jasmine's front door, getting ready to knock, but the door swung open before she could. It opened so fast that it startled her a little bit. She had bags in her hands. They were full of the ingredients that she was going to need to make her special dishes for the gathering.

"What's up, sis?" Anthony greeted her when she walked inside.

"I can't call it," she replied.

"Y'all already jammin' I see. I heard the music as soon as I got out of the car."

"I'm trying to get the party started. Jas tells me that you ladies have a whole menu to prepare."

Candice laughed. "I'm going to try my best."

He took her bags out of her hands and carried them into the kitchen for her. "Your first guest has arrived," Anthony sang as he walked into the kitchen. Jasmine was standing over the sink washing the meat so that it would be ready whenever Anthony got ready to cook it.

"Hey, boo." Candice hugged Jasmine.

"What's up?"

"You are looking good today honey." Candice noticed that Jasmine was beginning to look more and more like her normal self. It had taken her awhile to bounce back since her son was born, but everything was coming along quite nicely.

"Thank you. Thank you. I'm feeling a little better too," Jasmine lied.

Jasmine had already decided that she wouldn't tell her friends about the incident at the grocery store. Ever since Tamika said to her what she did, she felt like her constant drama was causing a burden for everyone around her, and she didn't want to be "that girl." She didn't want to be the one that brought everyone down all the time or the one that always had something wrong with her. She felt like as long as she was at home and Anthony was there, she would be okay, so she wanted to make the best of the day.

"Who all is coming over here today?" Candice asked.

"Well, you, of course, Tamika, Jenna, Dre, my cousins, Meesha and Myra, and their boyfriends, Rayshaun and Lamont."

"Oh, that's what's up. I haven't seen them since your baby shower."

"Me either, although I've spoken to them on the phone a few times since then. We agreed that since it's not that many of us cousins that we should try to make a conscious effort to spend more time together. I felt like this would be a good time so that everybody had somebody to talk to and nothing would seem forced. You know we were all close as kids, but when we grew up we grew apart. We've been trying to get together for the longest, but something always happens, and we can't"

"Hey! Hey! Hey! Hey!"

The girls heard a loud cheer. They turned around to see DeAndre walking through the kitchen's open entryway with his arms up like he was ready for a party. Jasmine smiled and spoke. She looked over at Candice, and Candice rolled her eyes at Jasmine. Jasmine thought that it was funny that Candice was acting like a child because she had finally realized that she had feelings for DeAndre. It wasn't like she had never had a boyfriend. She just hadn't had one in a very long time.

DeAndre put his bag down on the kitchen counter and walked over to Candice.

"Hey, Candice," he said, holding his arms open for a hug. He knew that Candice liked him because if she didn't, she would have rejected him when he kissed her on Jasmine's balcony, and she would have said something when he kissed her in Jasmine's kitchen. He also knew that she was nervous, and as bad as he wanted her, he knew that he couldn't rush her into anything because he didn't want to turn her off by being pushy.

"I guess I'll let you ladies get back to work. Can you put this in the refrigerator for me please?" he asked, referring to the bag he sat down on the counter.

"There is no reason why you should be turning colors when that man comes around you. What the hell is going on?" Jasmine asked.

"What do you mean?"

"Whenever he comes around you, you start blushing and turning all red. You act like you ain't never been around him before. You are really trippin'."

"I just be getting a lil' nervous. That's all. I don't know

why, but whatever. I didn't say anything to you when you sat down at Creve Coeur Park and expressed to me how you felt about Anthony, telling me about the butterflies and all that whenever you got around him."

"See, that's why you can't tell nobody nothing, 'cause they throw it back in your face," Jasmine said, throwing an oven mitt across the kitchen at Candice.

Anthony walked through the kitchen to get to the patio. As soon as the girls heard him coming, they stopped talking. He noticed that the mood in the room changed, so he stopped for a second and looked at both of them. Whenever he looked at one, that person would turn away like they didn't even notice him. He wanted to ask them what they were talking about before he came in the room, but he changed his mind and went outside where DeAndre was sitting.

When Anthony went outside and closed the patio door, Candice and Jasmine laughed so hard. They knew that he wanted to say something, but they were glad that he didn't because then they would have to lie.

"The girls are in there acting crazy, man," Anthony

told DeAndre.

"I know. They are in there talking about me," he told him.

"What makes you think they are talking about you?" Anthony asked, skeptical that they were actually in there talking about him of all people.

"Candice is feelin' yo' boy. She won't tell me, though. I heard them in there talking. I guess they thought that the door was closed all the way, but it wasn't. I already know that she likes me. She just keeps fighting it," he confessed.

"So they don't know you know?"

"They know that I know that Candice has a thing for me, but they don't know that I just heard them talking about it."

Anthony looked over at the girls in the kitchen and laughed because they thought that they were keeping something from him, but he knew more than they thought he did.

Just as Jasmine was about to go outside to hand Anthony a plate of meat to put on the grill, the doorbell rang. Candice ran to answer the door. She looked through the peephole and saw a few faces that she recognized. She opened the door and greeted each one of Jasmine's cousins with a hug. Jasmine went into the room where they were so that she could welcome them. One of them had two bottles of wine, and another one had a cake decorated beautifully in an elegant looking cake dish.

"Come on this way, guys. You can hang out in the kitchen with us or go hang out with the guys out back," Jasmine told them. The men went outside with the other men while the women stayed in the kitchen with Jasmine and Candice. Jasmine gave Meesha and Myra a rundown of what she and Candice were cooking in case they wanted to help. Candice decided to extend her hospitality and go out on the patio and offer the men an ice cold beer. Anthony laughed at her because although she offered one to everyone, she only looked at DeAndre when she offered it.

"Yes, Candice. I'll take a beer. Thank you very much," Anthony said loud enough to get her attention.

"See, what I tell you?" DeAndre asked Anthony.

Candice snapped her neck back. "What did you tell

him?" she asked.

"Don't trip. It's man business," DeAndre told her just to make her mind wonder.

She rolled her eyes and went back in the house after handing the beers over to Rayshaun and Lamont. She was still wondering about what it was that DeAndre told Anthony. It couldn't have been anything bad, or at least that's what she thought.

Jasmine, Meesha, Myra, and Candice did a lot talking about everything. Jasmine enjoyed the time that she was given to catch up with her cousins. It had been a minute since they got together, so she loved every minute of their company. They came and pitched right in with helping out in the kitchen, which, of course, made the cooking portion of the afternoon go by so much quicker. They appreciated that. None of them really wanted to spend the whole afternoon slaving in the kitchen. Meesha and Myra took turns playing with Malcolm. They were so excited to finally see him. Nobody knew it yet, but Jasmine had planned for everybody to join in and play some games together, but they were all couple games. She thought that the games would help with getting Candice and DeAndre to communicate more since Candice seemed to have gone into a shell ever since she realized she had feelings for the man. Jasmine thought that was backward; she should have gotten closer to him.

Anthony and DeAndre took turns on the grill. They both thought they had skills on the barbecue grill, so they had to show off. Anthony gave Rayshaun the remote to the stereo system and told him to find some music for everybody to listen to. He always did his best to make everyone feel comfortable and at home. If he felt like they were good people and he thought they would be around for awhile, he welcomed them in like family.

The girls brought some of the food out and arranged it neatly on the table so that everybody could start making their plates. Rayshaun had "Rock with You" by Michael Jackson playing through the speakers. Meesha and Myra brought out another round of beers for the guys and poured glasses of wine for all of the girls.

"I just realized that Tamika hasn't shown up yet. Has anyone heard from her today?" Jasmine asked.

Everyone told her no. Candice had actually forgotten that Tamika was supposed to come to the gathering. She was having such a good time without her and her negativity there, it hadn't even crossed her mind.

"I'll call her. At least we can make sure that nothing happened to her."

Jasmine went inside to get her phone. She dialed Tamika's number and waited for an answer, but she never got one. She hung up and dialed her phone number again. After several rings, she still didn't get an answer. She didn't bother calling her again. She went back to enjoying herself with the people that did show up.

When Jasmine noticed that everybody was finishing up their food, she changed the music on the radio to "The Wobble." She wanted to play something that would get everybody up and moving so that they could get ready to play one of her games. When the girls heard the song come on, they immediately went out on the lawn and began to do the dance that corresponded with that song. They guys didn't join in; they just sat back and watched the girls do their dance. The doorbell rang, and Anthony ran to see who it was. When he opened the door, it was Jenna.

"I didn't think you were going to come. I think you are the last person that we were waiting on because Jasmine couldn't get in touch with Tamika. The girls are all out back dancing. The food is out there too. Help yourself."

"Good, I'm starving. I had to work a double, and I just got off work. I worked through my lunch and haven't eaten all day."

They both walked toward the back. When Jasmine looked up and saw Jenna, she smiled and waved, but she didn't miss a step. Jenna took Anthony up on his offer and made her a plate after greeting the other guests that were there.

"Come on, y'all. Let's play a game," Jasmine announced. She thought that the guys would oppose, but to her surprise, they were all for it.

"The first game I want to play is 'Who Knows Best.' The purpose of the game is to find out how much you know about your mate."

"That's not fair. I don't have a mate, and Jenna doesn't either," Candice fussed.

"You pair up with Dre, and Jenna, can you read off the questions?" Jasmine replied.

"Me and DeAndre aren't even a couple. We are not going to be able to answer these questions accurately. What else can we play?"

"I have other games planned, but I want to play this one first," Jasmine persisted.

Jenna agreed to play host while everyone received the supplies they would need to play the game. Candice was shocked at how many things DeAndre actually knew about her. She didn't know as many things about him, but she didn't do that bad either. They did just as well with each other as the couples that had spent years together. That was all apart of Jasmine's plan, though. She wanted them to see how compatible they were.

After that, Jasmine set up a game for them to play where all of the couples had to go against each other and separate an entire bag of skittles by color. The first couple that finished won. Candice and DeAndre did not win, but they were able to work together and displayed great team work.

The last game they played was "How Much Can Your Man Carry?" Each of the women had to throw their men ten balls, and whichever man was able to carry the most amount of balls without dropping them, won that game. Candice and DeAndre won. Candice was excited to finally win one that she excitedly planted a kiss right on DeAndre's lips in front of everyone. He was totally caught off guard, but he wasn't mad about it. Jasmine, Jenna, and Anthony stood there with their mouths wide open. They couldn't believe that she did it either.

It seemed like Malcolm started whining just in time to give Candice a reason to excuse herself. She used the sleeve of her shirt to wipe her mouth and walked past DeAndre to check on Malcolm leaving everyone else there to try to figure out what had happened. DeAndre looked over at Anthony and gave him a look that said "I told you so." Anthony believed him when he told him earlier. Besides, he caught them kissing on the balcony at Jasmine's old apartment, but he didn't know it was that deep.

Jasmine, Jenna, Myra, and Meesha all went into the

house and left the guys outside.

"What did I miss?" Jenna asked. She was out of the loop. She had no idea that Candice and DeAndre liked each other.

Jasmine gave her the 4-1-1 while Meesha and Myra listened in. It wasn't a whole lot to tell, but it was interesting. Of course, girls loved that kind of gossip, so they all took it all in. Jasmine took Malcolm away from Candice and excused herself so that she could cater to him. The other girls headed back outside, but before they could get out there, Anthony was already bringing the food and other things back in.

"The party's over already?" Jenna asked.

"No, it's getting chilly out there, so we are moving everything inside," he told her.

Lamont and Rashaun were also carrying some things in, and DeAndre was too. When he walked in the door, he purposely bumped into Candice. He tried anything to give her a reason to say something to him. Instead of being adults about this whole thing, they both continued to act like teenagers that were crushing on each other.

After a few more beers and a little more girl chat, they decided to call it a night. Everybody said their goodbyes and went on their way. Usually, Candice and DeAndre would have stayed and helped clean up. but they both ended up leaving. Candice used the excuse of just being tired, and DeAndre claimed he had something to do. Anthony and Jasmine gave them both the side eye, not believing what either of them said, but they let it go. They cleaned up the mess on their own.

"I really enjoyed myself tonight," Jasmine said. It had been a long time since she enjoyed a night like that. The people were great, the food was great, and the energy was wonderful. She was low key happy that Tamika didn't show up. She felt like she probably would have put a damper on the mood.

"Your cousins and their friends were really nice. I'm glad you put this gathering together. I can't believe Candice and Dre. They are out of control. They probably need to just do it already and get it over with," Anthony told her while he was putting the leftover food away.

"Don't say that, Anthony. Why do they have to do it?"

"Because that's what they want to do. The sexual tension is there. It might be more to it than that, but right now, they need to knock the boots and then see if it's anything else after that 'cause they are just going to waste time playing around with each other."

"I can't believe you," Jasmine told him, shaking her head.

"I'm just saying."

When everything was cleaned and put away they headed upstairs to call it a night. Anthony put Malcolm to sleep, then he and Jasmine took turns washing each other in the shower and went to bed. Jasmine wanted to make love to him, but she was too tired, so she settled for a night of cuddling instead.

CHAPTER FOURTEEN

Jasmine and her friends were supposed to go over wedding details the night of her gathering, but they cut everything short and left before they could get to it. She had already hired vendors and put a down payment down for her venue, but when she thought about it, she decided that she didn't want all of that. She had planned for a beautiful garden wedding and an outdoor reception. She even hired her own personal bartender that agreed to create a signature drink for the occasion. She had a dress picked out and paid for, but she didn't want that either.

She called Jenna, Candice, and Tamika to let them know that she didn't want to go through with any of the plans that they once agreed upon. She knew that they would think she was crazy for wasting the money that she already spent and couldn't get back, but she didn't care about that. She really didn't want them to be upset about wasting so much time helping her with all the plans they had already made. They spent whole weekends cake tasting, searching for just the right venue, dress fittings, and menu planning for the reception, but it all began to get overwhelming for her, and she didn't want any of that anymore. It seemed like everything was getting too big. She originally wanted a big wedding, but in reality, there wouldn't be a lot of people there to enjoy it, so it started to seem pointless.

"Well, if you are not going to get married at the venue that you already chose, where are you going to get married?" Candice asked her, slightly frustrated at all of the changes. She would never tell her friend that she was getting on her nerves being so indecisive, but she most definitely was.

"You know, the ocean is really pretty, and it's been such a long time since any of us have been out of St. Louis," she hinted.

"What are you saying, Jay?" Jenna asked her.

"I think I want to get married on the beach."

"It's your choice. I just need to know what we are doing so that I can plan accordingly," Candice told her.

"Tamika, will you be able to make it?" Jasmine asked noticing how quiet she was.

"Of course, I'll be there."

"When do you want to do this, Jasmine? Will the date stay the same?" Candice asked.

"I was thinking next weekend."

"What? Now you know that's too short notice. How can we plan a wedding that quick?" Candice told her.

"I think you could make it work if you really tried," Jasmine responded, trying to convince her friends that it was possible.

"Have you asked Anthony how he feels about it yet?" Tamika asked her.

"Nope. You guys are the first. I just came up with the idea, but he said that he's down for whatever I wanted to do."

"Yeah, but that was before you decided to go all the way to the beach."

"Where exactly are we going, your majesty?" Tamika asked her.

"The Bahamas. I figured it's not too drastic. It's close and simple, and it should be a lot of fun for all of us," she replied ignoring Tamika's smart comment.

"Well, I don't think it's all that close, but I'm down," Jenna told her.

"Count me in. I need to get the hell out of here anyway. It's been way too long," Candice told her.

"Well, I guess that settles it," Tamika said.

Jasmine was ecstatic that everyone agreed to go. Before she called them, she wasn't sure how they were going to respond. She knew that it was short notice, but she also knew that it would be easy getting Anthony on board. He gave her her way all the time. It was the girls that would give her a hard time.

When she got off the phone with them, she danced around her bedroom with excitement.

"I'm getting married in the Baha-mas, I'm getting married in the Baha-mas, " she sang around the room. Even though she knew that he was going to be cool with it, she still had to tell him first. She went downstairs to find Anthony so that she could fill him in on her new plans.

After she told Anthony, she put her new plans in motion. She went shopping for everything that she thought they would need on their trip. She had to keep in mind that it wasn't just a vacation but her wedding, so she had to get things for that as well. When she told Anthony, he didn't mind the changes or the fact that some of his money had been wasted. He just told her the same thing that he always did, which is that he just wants her to be happy, so whatever was going to make her happy, he was going to do.

It seemed like when she got into the stores, her excitement took over. She didn't even know that she had it in her to shop the way she did before she got with Anthony. Maybe it was because she never had the unlimited funds to do it like she did now. Anthony just gave her a credit card or cash and told her to get what she wanted for her, the baby, or the house. Before him, she didn't have it that way. She always lived on a budget, not a strict budget, but she had to be mindful of the money she was spending. She couldn't even bring a lot of new stuff in the house at one time because Corey would swear that it came from another man. He didn't want her to be able to splurge on herself from time to time.

She knew she had to prepare well and get everything

done that needed to be done for this trip because her friends weren't going to stand for too many more changes. She had made enough and ran them around enough. She knew they were getting sick of her. She didn't even want to involve them in any more of the planning; she just did it all on her own. It was a lot of work for such a short time, but she did it. She worked throughout the entire week to get everything together, including making last minute reservations for their resort and airfare.

Anthony told her that whenever she got everything planned to let him know so that he could do what he wanted to do for her. He didn't care where they went. He already had in mind a few surprises that he wanted to have for her when they arrived. That just excited her even more. She couldn't wait to see what he had in store for her. He was always full of surprises. She just didn't know what he could possibly do to top all that he had done already.

CHAPTER FIFTEEN

The time had flown by so fast, and Jasmine couldn't believe that she, Anthony, and Malcolm were headed to the Bahamas already, but the day finally arrived for them to fly out. While Anthony didn't seem bothered by anything or anyone, Jasmine's nerves were getting the best of her. She started to feel silly for rushing things. She began to think that she could have waited a little bit longer, but it was too late. She knew that she loved Anthony without a doubt, but now that the time was drawing closer to finally tie the knot, she couldn't help but get cold feet. She kind of felt guilty about feeling the way she was, but it was nothing she could do about it. She tried to reassure herself time and time again that it was what she had waited so long for, and it was what she needed to officially complete her family.

DeAndre dropped the three of them off at the airport. Jasmine and Anthony had to arrive at the Bahamas a few days before everyone else to prepare for the big day, but the rest of the crew was due to arrive shortly after. It took them forever to get to the airport because Jasmine kept doing a bag check. She was afraid that she might leave something important behind. She would first count all the bags. She knew exactly how many bags each person was supposed to have, and she even had everyone's luggage color coded. Then, she would have to look inside the bags to make sure everything was inside of them that she wanted. Anthony thought that she was losing her mind, but he just let her do whatever she needed to do to ease her nerves a little bit.

After the truck was unloaded, they both thanked DeAndre for the ride and said their goodbyes. It seemed like it took them forever to get through security and to get their bags checked. By the time they were done, they made it to their gate just in time to board their flight, which was kind of a relief because they didn't have to wait around. They were continuously moving. Jasmine had never flown with a baby before, so she didn't know what to expect. She remembered all of the articles she'd read or videos she'd watched of parents being kicked off of an airplane because their baby kept crying, and they had two flights to catch before getting to their destination. Anthony kept trying to assure her that everything would be okay, and she didn't have anything to worry about.

Jasmine found her seat and settled in with the baby while Anthony put his diaper bag in the overhead compartment. He took his seat next to his fiancée and grabbed her hand.

"Everything is going to be fine, Jay," he told her. He could look at her and still see the wheels spinning in her head. He thought that she was going to drive herself crazy before he even had a chance to marry her.

Before Anthony let her hand go, she closed her eyes and said a silent prayer for a safe flight. She forgot to do that before she left the house.

"Amen. Now, relax and get some rest," Anthony told her when she finished her prayer.

She took his advice and pulled out a book with crossword puzzles. She needed something to ease her mind. By the time the wheels on the plane went up, Anthony was already dozing off. She looked over at him and wondered how he could be so calm through all of this.

She wondered if he had any nervousness or cold feet and was just playing it off so that she wouldn't suspect it. He was so sure of himself, and that too made her feel nervous. She was just a wreck. She laid her head back against the seat while her son laid on her chest. She slowly rubbed his back while he slept and that helped her to relax a little bit.

Well, this is it. I'm leaving St. Louis with a fiancé, and I'll come back with a husband, she thought to herself. *This could only be the beginning of great things to come.*

The butterflies started to subside in her stomach a little bit. She knew that she was doing the right thing. It was nothing that could make this situation more right. He was a great man to her and an even better father to her son that wasn't even his. He was there for her a hundred percent throughout her entire pregnancy. He didn't care about the fact that she was carrying another man's baby, and if he did, he didn't show it. She was proud to have him by her side and in her life. Just a few months ago, you couldn't tell her that her life would turn around so drastically. She wouldn't have believed it.

Anthony grabbed Jasmine's hand and kissed it.

"I thought you were sleep."

"I tried to fall asleep, but I couldn't."

"Are you okay?" she asked him, hoping that he wasn't starting to get cold feet too.

"I'm fine, Jas. I just want you to be okay. You seem real nervous, and I don't want you to rush into something that you are not ready for. Marriage is a one-time thing for me, baby. And once we say 'I do,' I won't be willing to let you go, so I need you to be sure that this is what you want. If we need to, we can postpone this trip and go back home," he said sincerely.

Jasmine's heart raced when those words came out of his mouth. She didn't expect him to sense her nervousness about getting married. She knew that he knew that she was nervous about traveling but not getting married. It kind of made her feel bad because now, he thought that she didn't want to marry him.

"Anthony, I want to marry you. I just don't want you to marry me and change your mind later, or what if I have more babies, and my body doesn't go back to what it is now, and you start to find me unattractive? I don't want you to cheat on me or dog me out because I'm not the same person that you fell in love with."

Anthony sat up in his seat and looked at Jasmine, peeping the look of confusion all over her face. He had no idea that she felt that way. It kind of upset him to know that she thought that he would be that shallow.

"Jasmine, you are worried about the wrong things, baby. Look at you. You don't look like you did when I first met you. You were a teenager, baby. You are a grown woman now. You have already had a baby, and your body has already changed, and I'm still here. I love you, I love your body, and I expect you to change. I don't expect you to stay the same forever, and I'm sure I won't either. I hope you don't dip when I start to change, and for you to think I'd cheat on you is messed up. After all these years, I came back to you, baby. Can't no other woman touch my heart like you have. You don't have to worry about that. Now, are we going to do this, or what?"

Jasmine had tears in her eyes, but she didn't let one fall. After Anthony professed his love to her, she was convinced that she was making the right decision. Nobody had ever made her feel like he did. As much as she thought she loved Corey and as many ass whoopings that she took from him and stayed because he said that he loved her too, she knew now what true love was, not just with what Anthony said to her but because of the way he treated her. He always treated her with respect, and he always made her feel like she was the only woman in the room even if there were fifty other women. She always had his undivided attention, and he didn't abuse her physically.

"We're doing this," she told him with a smile on her face.

"That's what I was hoping to hear. You had me nervous, Jay. I was sure of us getting married until I started to see how nervous you were. I thought you were gone flake on me," he told her.

"I'm all in, Anthony," she told him.

He leaned over and kissed her on her lips. He rested his head on the back of his seat and leaned it back a little. They both were able to enjoy the rest of the flight in peace knowing how each of them felt about taking this next step in their lives together.

CHAPTER SIXTEEN

Excitement filled the room, and the feeling of eagerness filled Jasmine's heart. The day had finally come to marry the man that she had loved ever since she was a teenage girl. She had her girls surrounding her in her suite that she rented for the entire bridal party to prepare for the big day.

Candice, Tamika, and Jenna were very supportive and helpful in keeping Jasmine together and her emotions in check, although at different parts throughout the day she would burst out in tears for no reason that anyone could pinpoint. They just thought that she was emotional because she was getting married.

A knock at the door startled the girls, and their conversation came to a pause.

"Are you expecting anybody, Jasmine?" Candice inquired.

"No. Not this early," she told her.

Candice looked through the peephole on the door of the suite to see who it was, but she didn't know any of the people on the other side of the door.

"Girl, it's four men out there," Candice whispered.

All of the girls stood at attention.

"I know y'all didn't call no strippers all the way out here," Jasmine said.

"Girl, you know we didn't call no strippers all the way to the Bahamas."

"Well, who are they?"

"Shit, I don't know."

"Answer it. Why y'all acting so scary?" Jenna asked them.

"I ain't scary. I just don't know these men, and nobody should know that we are here," Candice replied.

"I got this," Jenna told them before going to the door.

Candice stepped back, and Jenna opened the door.

"May I help you?" she gracefully asked.

"Is this the room of Jasmine Washington?" one of the guys asked.

"It is. What can we help you with?" she asked again but this time not so nice.

"We were sent here to give her and her friends the time

of their lives," one of the other guys spoke up.

"What the hell?" Candice asked.

"Are you strippers?" Jenna asked.

"No. We were sent here by Anthony. He wanted us to give his fiancée and her friends full body massages while getting ready for the ceremony."

"Oh okay. Well, I guess you can set up over there," Jenna told them, using her hands to gesture to them where they could set up their massage tables.

All of the girls exchanged looks with each other as the guys walked in carrying their tables over to where Jenna told them to set up.

"I don't feel comfortable with this," Jasmine told them.

"I can't get naked in front of these men that I don't know."

"Shit, if you were at a spa, you would be naked in front of someone you don't know. At least you have all of us here. You're not by yourself," Candice told Jasmine.

"Look here, I'm getting this massage," Tamika said while checking the men out, trying to figure out which one she wanted to massage her.

"I'll be right back," Jasmine told her friends.

She walked into the bathroom in the suite and took her cell phone out of the pocket of her silk robe.

"Anthony, where are you?" Jasmine asked him when he answered his phone.

"I'm at the hotel with the fellas. Is everything okay?"

"I don't know. Some guys just showed up to my room. They said that you sent them here to give us full body massages," Jasmine whispered into the phone.

"Oh yeah, they're cool. I sent them. They are already paid for up to two hours for each of you. Get a glass of wine, and enjoy yourself."

Jasmine managed to let a smile spread across her face. She didn't feel so nervous anymore since she knew the guys were legit.

"Okay, Ant. I was just making sure everything was okay."

"You're in good hands, baby. I'll see you in a few hours."

"Okay. Love you."

"Love you too."

Jasmine ended the call on her phone and joined her friends.

"Okay, Jasmine. Although we already know who we want, we decided to let you choose first because it's your special day. Which guy do you want?" Jenna asked.

Jasmine smiled and looked at all the guys. This was very exciting for her because she was usually so conservative. She felt like she was picking a man for all the wrong reasons, but she was willing to do it.

"I'll pick him," Jasmine pointed to the guy with the chocolate complexion. She had already checked him out when he first came into the room. He had a muscular build that was just right. She didn't like her men too bulky, he wore his hair cut down low, and his waves were popping. When she was able to catch him smiling, she noticed how pretty his teeth were. He just had her intrigued from the time he came through the door.

"I knew you would pick him," Tamika told her.

"Well, you know me well," she replied.

The girls had already been walking around the suite in their silk robes, so the only thing they had to do was take them off and get on the tables.

"Okay, ladies, we are all ready when you are. Would you like for us to step out of the room so that you can get yourselves comfortable on the tables? Or we can just stand over here and turn around," one of the massage therapists said.

"We'll be fine with you just turning around," Jasmine spoke up for all of the girls.

The four guys walked over to the window and turned their backs to the girls.

Jasmine, Tamika, Candice, and Jenna slid under the sheets that were draped across their tables and laid their faces in the face cradles.

"We're ready," Candice told them.

The guys took their position at their individual tables and gave each other a look to indicate that they were ready. One of the guys cued the music, and they all got to work.

From the first touch, Jasmine trembled. Anthony had been the only man to touch her in awhile. It was weird to her to have another man touching on her, but it sure did feel good.

Tamika moaned as her guy rubbed her neck and shoulders. His touch was taking her mind in places that she knew it shouldn't go, but she didn't care. She let her mind drift off. Candice fell asleep almost instantly, and Jenna was just relaxed and taking it all in.

Jasmine couldn't help but think about her fiancé and how much he really loved her. The things that he did for her on a daily basis were amazing. She wished that she would have been exposed to a love like his so much sooner. She knew that she deserved it after all that she had been through. She let her thoughts of Anthony sink in until she drifted off.

She slept through the first part of the massage until her therapist whispered in her ear that he needed her to turn over.

She almost forgot where she was. When she felt his warm breath in her ear and heard his voice, she opened her eyes but didn't look up until it clicked in her mind what was going on. He lifted the sheet just enough for her to turn over and when she did, she looked up at him and smiled.

He draped the sheet and tucked it underneath her arms

and legs. She watched him as he walked to the foot of the table and began to rub her feet. That was a sensitive spot for her. A man touching her feet always turned her on. She bit her bottom lip and closed her eyes as he worked his magic on her. He smiled knowing that he was pleasing his client.

Jasmine looked over at her friends to see if they were enjoying their massages just as much as she was. They seemed to be. Candice was snoring, and Tamika was constantly moaning almost every time the man touched her. Jenna looked pretty relaxed as well.

"Okay, ladies, our time is up," Tamika's therapist announced.

"Aw man, I was just starting to doze back off," Jasmine said.

"Well, we will be available to work on you all again. Just give us a call and set up an appointment."

"So, what? You're not from here?" Tamika asked.

"No, we're not from the Bahamas. We are from St. Louis too," one of the guys said.

"It was nice of you guys to come all the way out here

just to give us massages."

"It's our job, and Anthony paid for the trip, so we couldn't turn him down."

Jasmine looked around at everything and everybody that surrounded her at that moment. She knew that Anthony had money, but she never knew how much money. She wondered how he was able to put her and her friends up in their expensive suite in the Bahamas, pay for four men to come all the way to the Bahamas, and pay for massages. Not to mention, he was paying for the whole wedding and the rest of the vacation. He was just going all out.

"Do you always work together?"

"We cater to the client, so if you want a group session like today, we'll do it... if you want a personal session, that's an option too."

"We'll step into the hallway and let you take your time getting dressed, and you can let us in to get our things when you are done."

The men walked out of the room and stepped into the hallway.

The four girls stretched and neither of them could seem to wipe the smiles off of their faces. They were really relaxed.

"I think I could lay here forever," Jasmine said.

"Well, too bad you have a wedding to get ready for. We only have a few hours left to pull everything together," Candice said, throwing a towel at Jasmine.

Candice was the maid of honor, and she was taking her role seriously. She made an extra effort to make sure that everything was how and where it should be, and she wanted to make sure that everybody stayed on task and on schedule. She couldn't do anything about the massages taking up two hours of their time because she didn't know they were coming, but it was well worth it.

Moaning and groaning not wanting to get up, Tamika got up and wrapped her robe around her. Jenna did the same, and Jasmine continued to lie there.

Candice walked over to Jasmine and pulled her off the table by her arms and made her stand to her feet. She handed Jasmine her robe and tied it after Jasmine put it on.

"It's a dog on shame. I have to dress you like a baby,"

Candice fussed.

"I wasn't ready for him to stop," Jasmine whined.

"That was so nice of Anthony to do that for us," Jenna said.

Tamika walked over to the door to let the guys back in after everybody was covered.

"Thank you again. I didn't catch your name." Jasmine extended her hand to her massage therapist.

"My name is Donavan." He gently grabbed her hand and thanked her for the opportunity to work on her.

"You enjoy the rest of your day," he told her.

"Thank you," she replied and walked away.

She went to get some things out of one of her bags. When she looked up, she saw the girls conversing with their therapists. Tamika's fast ass was putting her phone number in her massage therapist's phone, and he was putting his number in her phone.

"Alright, y'all, I'm going to take a shower before Kat get's here," Jasmine yelled out.

"Who is Kat?" Tamika asked.

"You ain't never heard of Kat? She goes by Kat

Mahogany Sanders. She's a dope ass makeup artist. I fell in love with her work when I saw her Facebook page. I reached out to her, and she said that she'd do my makeup for the wedding."

"That's what's up. Well, we'll make sure these guys get out safely, and you finish doing what you have to do," Tamika replied.

Jasmine proceeded to the bathroom to finish getting herself prepared for the next phase of her process.

Candice let Jenna and Tamika do what they were doing. She didn't have time to flirt with the guys any longer. She dismissed herself and went to check her list of things that still needed to be done. It wasn't much left, but she didn't want to leave anything out.

"Okay, ladies, we have everything. We'll see you soon," one of the guys said before they all walked out of the door.

The girls didn't bother seeing them to the door. They waved bye and sat down.

"This has been a long day already, and the ceremony hasn't even started," Tamika complained.

"That massage didn't make it any better either. I'm ready for a nap now," Jenna chimed in.

Jasmine emerged from the bathroom and saw everybody relaxing.

"What's next on the list?" she asked Candice.

"You're waiting for Kat to arrive, and your hair stylist should be here soon. Your dress has been delivered, and we just have to get you in it," Candice informed her.

Jasmine was tired, but she was running off of her reserved adrenaline. Just as she sat down getting ready to indulge in a cup of tea, there was a knock on the door.

Candice ran to the door and asked who it was. Jasmine couldn't hear what the person on the other side of the door said, but when the door opened up and she saw Kat standing there, she jumped out of her chair and ran to hug her.

"I'm so happy you were able to make it," she said full of excitement.

"Me too, girl. I'm so excited for this wedding," Kat told her.

Jasmine helped Kat get her things out of the hallway.

She came prepared for the job. It didn't look like she left any supplies back home. She knew that Kat was going to get her right. She was a dope, self-made makeup artist. Her prices were reasonable, and she left her clients satisfied.

"Will I be doing everyone's makeup or just yours?"

Jasmine looked around at her girls. "Do you guys want her to hook you up? I'll pay for it." Jenna and Candice jumped at the chance to get their faces beat by Kat. They had heard so much about her that they had to take advantage of the opportunity.

"Yeah, hook me up," Candice replied.

"Me too," Jenna agreed.

"I'm good," Tamika said.

Candice looked at Tamika and shook her head. There was nothing she could say or at least nothing she could say that wouldn't ruin Jasmine's big day. They all took turns letting Kat work her magic on each of them. Tamika sat in the corner and did her own makeup and got a head start on her hair.

"Kat, she looks so pretty," Candice said when she looked over at her friend.

"You do look really good," Kat agreed.

She was performing some finishing touches on Jasmine's makeup just as someone came and knocked on the door.

Jenna opened it up to see a short brown skinned girl carrying an oversized duffle bag.

"Hey, Monica, girl," Candice said excitedly when she looked up and saw the hairstylist at the door.

"Just in time. I'm done with you. When she finishes setting her things up, you can go to her," Kat said.

"Thank you so much," Jasmine said, giving her a hug.

Candice sat down at the table when Jasmine got up. Candice was more than ready to have her makeup done. The girls rotated around the room like they were playing musical chairs until everyone was taken care of. When the time came for Jasmine to put on her dress, everybody helped. It wasn't a big dress, but they had to make sure that she didn't mess up her hair and makeup.

"We have to head down in about ten minutes," Candice called out to the group. All of the girls finished with their last minute things. Even Kat and the hairstylist stayed with them to help with whatever they may have needed help with. Before leaving the suite, Jenna called everybody to gather around so that she could say a prayer with them. She wanted to pray for Jasmine and her marriage, she wanted to pray for the rest of their day to go smoothly, and she just wanted to thank God for bringing them as far as they had come. Everybody gathered in a circle and held hands so that Jenna could lead them in prayer. When she was done, there wasn't one dry eye in the room.

"Aw man, Jenna. We might have to get our makeup redone," Jasmine whined.

"Nope. You girls are fine," Kat told them after giving them a once over.

Jasmine took one more look at herself in the mirror and headed out of the door of her suite, and everyone followed behind her.

Candice snuck a quick text to Anthony to let him know that they were on their way down so that he could make sure he was nowhere around. She didn't want him to accidentally see Jasmine before it was time. Anthony made sure that they both got the most expensive suites at the resort, but they were not to see each other until the ceremony. When he got the text, he called for his half of the wedding party to get in position. He couldn't believe that this thing was starting on time. It usually took them forever to get ready for a regular night out on the town, so he knew for sure they were going to be late for his wedding too. He even paid for a little extra time just in case they were, but to his surprise, they weren't. *I guess she just couldn't wait to marry big daddy,* he said to himself.

When Jasmine reached the beach entrance, she stopped in her tracks. Her heart was racing, and she started to feel a little panicked. She wasn't having cold feet; she was just overwhelmed. She turned around and looked at her friends, and they gave her a nod of approval. No one that knew Jasmine could think of her being with anyone but Anthony. They knew that she was making the right decision, and she had come too far to turn away.

She continued on to the beach where there was a vehicle there waiting for them to take them closer to where her ceremony was to take place. Everybody loaded up in the vehicle, and they were on their way. When they arrived, they made sure to stay a few feet away so they could get situated. Everyone needed to get into place, and the DJ had to be cued for the music.

When the guys saw the girls arrive, the groomsman went to take their place with the bridesmaids, and Kat and the hairstylist took their seats with the rest of the friends and family. Chris, the guy that was assigned to walk with Jenna, held his hand out for her to hold, and they took their position in line. Justin, the guy that was assigned to walk with Tamika, followed suit and did the same thing. DeAndre held his hand out for Candice to take, and they took their position in the line as well. Jasmine stood in the back of the line, still nervous but ready. She made sure that they were dropped off far away enough that Anthony would not be able to get a good look at her before it was time. Her wedding party was small, just the way she wanted it. She didn't have a flower girl or a ring bearer.

The DJ played the instrumental to Jesse Powell's "You." That let the bridal party know that it was time for them to make their way down the aisle. First, Jenna and Chris went, followed by Justin and Tamika and then

DeAndre and Candice.

"You look so beautiful, C," DeAndre told Candice before they started down the aisle.

"Thank you, DeAndre. You don't look bad yourself."

Candice tried not to show too much emotion, but when she saw DeAndre for the first time in his wedding attire, her mind was blown. She had no idea he could clean up so well, or maybe he had before, and she just didn't pay him any attention. She was definitely starting to feel something for him, but she didn't want to show it. She wondered why whatever she was seeing in him now, she had never seen before. She managed to put her thoughts behind her so that she could make her way down the aisle.

When they finally made it to the front, it was Jasmine's turn. She stood in her position and waited for the music to change. When cued, the DJ switched the song to "Forever" by Jaheim. Jasmine walked down the aisle with so much grace and poise. She didn't have anybody to walk with her, and she didn't mind. Originally, DeAndre was going to walk her down the aisle, but she agreed to let him be Anthony's best man.

As she made her way toward her soon-to-be husband, she took in the breathtaking view of the ocean behind him. The water was so blue, and the waves and wind were so calming. She tried her best not to make eye contact with him because she knew that if she did, she would cry. She kept trying to look past him, but she couldn't stop paying attention to how good he looked in his attire. She checked out the entire wedding party, and everybody looked good. She was impressed at how the guys cleaned up because she was so used to seeing them in their street clothes. She wasn't sure if they would be able to pull it off. Even though they weren't dressed in tuxedos, they weren't in baggy pants and t-shirts either. She was happy that they didn't go with the traditional wedding attire. She figured that they didn't have to since the wedding was on the beach.

She wore a short, white dress with a coral colored belt and a beaded design on the top. It was sleeveless, and the bottom had poofy ruffles. Jenna, Tamika, and Candice all wore short, coral sleeveless dresses and coral hair accessories. The girls didn't want to go completely barefoot, so they wore foot jewelry. Jasmine liked the fact that they gave the illusion of shoes, even though they weren't. Anthony, DeAndre, and the groomsmen wore khaki shorts, short sleeve button up shirts, and all of their accessories were coral. Anthony was the only one that wore a hat, and his hat had a coral colored feather in it. He said that was his way of standing out from everybody else. Jasmine and her bridesmaids had coral and white bouquets that coordinated with everything else.

Almost at the end of the aisle, Jasmine saw the few friends and family members that she invited. She wasn't really close to a lot of her relatives, so she just kept her guests to the people that she dealt with often, and that wasn't a lot. It was the same thing with Anthony and his family. It wasn't a lot of them, but his main ones were there. When she got to the last row of chairs right before reaching the front where her bridal party waited for her, she stopped in her tracks. After all that time she fought her tears from being nervous and anxious about marrying Anthony, she couldn't fight her tears anymore. Her mother stood up and hugged her as tight as she could. She didn't even invite her mother because she knew it would be too hard for her to come. She just didn't know that no matter how sick her mother was, she wouldn't have missed her wedding for anything. Her mom broke their embrace and wiped the tears from her face.

"Go on up there and marry that man, baby," her mother whispered to her while wiping her own tears.

There wasn't a dry eye there, even the wedding officiant was caught shedding a tear or two. Jasmine walked over to Anthony and held his hand before looking up at him. "Thank you," she mouthed to him. He responded with a smile.

The two faced the officiant and proceeded with the ceremony. They both recited their own vows that they wrote and exchanged rings. They prayed over their unity sand display before pouring their coral and white colored sand in its vase. Jasmine originally wanted a unity candle, but she couldn't guarantee that it would be able to stay lit because of the wind, so she opted for the sand which she thought turned out to be very pretty.

When Anthony was finally allowed to kiss his bride, he took her in his arms and kissed her slowly. It was the moment that he waited for after so long. He didn't want to rush it. He was thrilled to be kissing his wife—Jasmine.

They held hands and finally, as a married couple, they walked down the sandy aisle, waving at their guests. The entire wedding party managed to slip away to take some pictures by the ocean. Anthony had hired and flew out a photographer that he met from back home. He couldn't trust just anybody with the most important pictures he'd ever take in his life. Jasmine even managed to get some pictures with her mother and her mother with her son. She cherished those moments more than anything.

For the next few hours, Jasmine, Anthony, and their friends and family partied on the beach underneath a rented tent until the sun began to set over the ocean. It was so beautiful. The last part of the reception was for the entire wedding party and guests to say a group prayer and have one last toast underneath the beautifully glowing sky.

When the toast was over, Jasmine turned to Anthony and gave him a passionate kiss right in front of everyone. She didn't care; she was tired of the little peck here and peck there. Anthony took that as a sign of Jasmine being ready to start their solo part of the night. He noticed how much champagne she drank that night, so he figured she was warmed up and ready to go.

They both thanked everyone for coming, they kissed Malcolm, and went on their way. Jasmine kind of felt bad for leaving everyone like they did, but they knew that it was part of the plan anyway. Candice and DeAndre would take care of Malcolm for the night so that Anthony and Jas could have their wedding night alone. Tamika and Jenna would probably be on the night prowl for some locals to hang with. She didn't even know her mom would be there, so she had no idea what she would do to stay busy for the rest of the night, but she hoped that she would find something to do. Their wedding guests planned to stay the next day and a half at the resort with them so that they could all kick it before they all went back home, but the night was for the newlyweds.

CHAPTER SEVENTEEN

Anthony picked Jasmine up and carried her over the threshold of their suite. He saw her eyes light up when they entered the room, and that was just in the entryway. He already had the honeymoon suite all set up for them. It was decorated with rose petals, chocolate candy, chocolate covered strawberries, lit candles all around the room, and more champagne. The honeymoon package that he purchased already came with some of these decoration options, but when they arrived, he secretly paid one of the workers to add a little extra to the room.

Like the heart in the center of the bed made out of rose petals with the initials A & J inside the heart. There were pictures of them all over the room from when they first started dating to now, and Anthony had a gift waiting for Jasmine on a nearby table. It was sitting in the center of a heart made of rose petals. She walked all around the room in awe of its beauty. She couldn't believe that Anthony had done all of this for her. She never had a man go to this extreme for her. She tried to walk through and not miss any details. Anthony stood back against a wall and watched her as she moved through the room. He smiled at her excitement about every little thing. She was like a kid in a toy store. Her continuous ooh's and ahh's let him know that he did a good job.

"Oooh Anthony, look at this big jacuzzi tub," she cheerfully expressed.

"I know" was all he said.

"These candles smell so good," she told him.

"It's all for you," he replied.

Jasmine sashayed over to him as he was still leaning against the wall and wrapped her arms around his neck. He leaned in for a kiss, but she began kissing his neck instead. She knew just the places to put her lips to turn him on the most. Anthony grabbed her underneath her thighs to lift her, she wrapped her legs around his waist, and he turned around to pin her against the wall. They kissed each other deeply.

A few minutes in, Anthony stopped and put her down.

"What's wrong Ant, why'd you stop?"

He walked her over to the table to sit down and didn't

say a word. She was confused, but she didn't say anything either. He walked over to where the champagne classes were and poured them both a glass of champagne.

"Let's make a toast." He handed her a glass, and they both took turns saying what they wanted to toast to. They tapped glasses, and they both guzzled the liquid down as if they were taking shots.

Anthony walked into the bathroom to draw a bath for he and Jasmine. He made sure to throw in some rose petals. The bathroom was covered with so many bouquets of roses it looked like they were in a garden. While Anthony was running bath water for them, Jasmine ate some of her chocolate covered strawberries. She watched him as he took his shirt off so that it wouldn't get wet. She had drank so much champagne at her reception that she was already hot. Everything he did at that moment turned her on.

While his back was turned to her, she slipped out of her dress and threw it on the floor. She sat back down in the chair with her legs spread apart and started to rub herself. She played with her pussy until it got wet. When she took her fingers out of her and saw her juices all over her fingers, she reached over and grabbed another strawberry. She seductively sucked all of the chocolate off of it and used it to spread her lips apart. At that point, she couldn't help it. She let out a soft moan that got Anthony's attention. He turned around to see what was going on.

"Jasmine, what are you doing?"

She didn't respond. She continued to rub her clitoris with the strawberry. Anthony started walking towards her, and she stuck the strawberry inside of her, covering it with her warm juices, and fed it to him. He didn't know what had gotten into Jasmine because he had never seen this side of her, but he was loving it. He got down on his knees and began to lick her lower lips. Jasmine threw her head back and moaned. She reached down and pushed his head so that he could stick his tongue further inside of her.

"Baby, I want to feel you," she moaned.

Her request fell on deaf ears. He didn't respond, and he didn't stop what he was doing. After awhile, Jasmine couldn't take it anymore, her body started to shake as she came. That still didn't make Anthony move.

"Oooh, Anthony, get up baby," she begged because he kept going, although she had gotten really sensitive down there.

Anthony stood up and unbuckled his belt. He let his pants fall to the floor. He picked Jasmine up and draped her legs over his arms, and while holding her, he eased his penis inside of her.

"Oh my God," she cried out. She tried to control herself. She didn't want to cum twice, and he hadn't cum at all yet. Jas bit her bottom lip as Anthony kept thrusting in and out of her. It didn't take long for both of them to cum. When they did, he lowered her onto the floor and grabbed her hand, pulling her toward the bathtub, where they did it again. Anthony wanted to make sure that Jasmine was satisfied before she went to bed that night.

After round two, they made their way to the bed and cleared it of all of the decorations that were neatly arranged on them. They thought they were going to get a round three, but they couldn't even hang that long. They passed out in the bed on top of the covers. Between the entire wedding ceremony, reception celebration, and the activities that had just taken place plus all of the alcohol they both consumed, they were beat.

Jasmine woke up in the middle of the night and called Candice. She wanted to check on Malcolm. She called her phone, but she didn't answer. She looked at her phone to make sure she dialed the right number. When she realized she had, she checked the clock to see what time it was. It was four in the morning, and she didn't necessarily expect for Candice to be awake, but she hoped that she would answer her call.

She couldn't get a hold of Candice, so she called her mom's cell phone. She knew that everybody else had somewhere to go after the wedding, but she didn't know where her mother was.

"Hey, Ma," she said when her mother answered the phone.

"What are you doing up? You sound wide awake," she told her mom.

"I always get up this early. You would know that if you called me more."

"I know. I'm sorry, Ma."

"I got up early to eat breakfast and to take a stroll along the beach. It's so beautiful out there," she told Jasmine.

"I know it is. Me and Anthony will be out there later."

"Jasmine, tend to your husband, baby. When you decide you're ready to come out, everybody will be ready for you. Don't rush for us. I want you to know that I am so proud of you. You have been through so much, and I don't know how you have gotten through all of it, but you have handled it with grace. You have a beautiful son, and you have such a good and respectable husband. You are a smart girl, and I know that when the time is right, you'll go back to school or do whatever you decide. Just make sure whatever you choose is for you, and that it makes you happy."

"I will, Mama. Thank you."

"I love you, Jasmine."

"I love you too, Mama," Jasmine said before hanging up her phone.

Jasmine crawled back in the bed and cuddled up under Anthony. She thought about everything that her mother said. She thought about going back to school one day, but she wasn't sure if she was going to actually do it, though. She figured that if she did, it wouldn't be for the same thing as before. She thought that she might want to go back and get her degree so that she could be some kind of therapist. She wanted to help women in abusive relationships. She figured she knew all about it, so it would be easy for her to mentor to those women. She also kind of wanted to work with children. She was still undecided, but she knew that she would eventually do something.

CHAPTER EIGHTEEN

Jasmine never really went back to sleep after she talked to her mother on the phone. She laid with Anthony for awhile and then got up to shower. When she got out of the shower she noticed that they hadn't brought their clothes over from the first suite they stayed in upon arriving to the Bahamas, so she called Jenna to bring her bags over to her, then she called DeAndre to bring Anthony's bags over for him.

When Jenna got to where Jasmine was staying, Jasmine was still wrapped up in her towel. She opened the door and invited her in.

"Good morning, Mrs. Williams," Jenna greeted her.

"Hey, girl," Jenna replied.

"This place is nice," Jenna told her, referring to the suite. Jenna didn't walk all the way through it, not wanting to invade their privacy, but the little bit that she saw was mind blowing.

"I said the same thing when I saw it. Although when I first saw it, it was covered in lit candles, rose petals, and some more stuff."

"That's what I'm talking about. Romance at it's finest."

"What did the rest of you end up doing last night?" Jasmine asked her.

"Candice and DeAndre sat out on the beach most of the night talking."

"Where was Malcolm?" Jasmine cut her off before she could finish.

"He was with them. Girl, they looked like a lil' family out there. Me and Tamika went to a local club and had a few more drinks and danced a little bit. It was really nice. I think everyone enjoyed themselves. Some of your wedding guests were there too. Everybody just kicked it."

"I'm glad everybody had fun. I definitely want to come back here again. Maybe on a girls' trip, a quick get away," Jasmine told her.

"What's up, Jenna?" Anthony said, peeking around the corner.

"Hey, Anthony," she replied.

"Well, yo' man is up now. I'll go and leave y'all

alone."

Before Jenna could get all the way out of the door, DeAndre was approaching with Anthony's things. He spoke to Jenna. She spoke back and went on her way. DeAndre looked at Jasmine. Even though he was feeling Candice now, he still thought Jasmine was beautiful. She was standing in the doorway with her hair blowing in the wind that was coming through. She went from friend, to sister, back to friend, and now, he was going to add the one that got away to that list too. He just wanted her to be happy regardless of who she ended up with. Because of her, he gained a brother and a nephew, and she was still in his life. That was enough for him.

"Thanks, Dre," Jasmine said as she reached out to grab the bags.

"No problem, Jay. How are you?" he asked.

"I'm fine."

"Well, everybody is trying to catch breakfast before we start our water activities. Do you think you and Ant will make it?"

"I already ordered room service. They should be here

shortly."

"Alright. Well, we'll see you guys when you are done," he told her. He left to go meet up with the rest of their friends.

Jasmine closed the door behind him and yelled out to Anthony that she had his clothes. He hadn't realized that he didn't have any clean clothes either. After he showered, they ate breakfast and got dressed for the day. They had activities planned for everyone. Some of their wedding guests stayed to spend some time with them as well. Jasmine's mom didn't want to participate in any of the activities, so she volunteered to take care of her grandson.

Jasmine and Anthony started off paddle boarding. Candice, DeAndre, Tamika, and Jenna took a boat ride. Tamika had been giving Candice and Dre the side eye for awhile now. She could tell that something was different about them. She noticed that they technically spent the whole night together, and now, they were sitting together on the boat.

"Y'all are mighty close," she told them with her lips curled up like something smelled bad.

"We are just sitting here talking," DeAndre told her.

"You two isolated yourselves from us like you wanted to be alone or something," she continued.

"I think you're reading too much into this, Tamika. We are just friends. You already know that."

"Uh un, I don't know anything," Tamika told her.

Frustrated with the interrogation, Candice jumped in, "If we were getting closer than usual, what would that mean to you?"

"It wouldn't mean nothing, except the fact that you are always talking that sister stuff, but you're keeping secrets from your sisters. If you like him, you like him."

"There aren't any secrets to be kept. Me and DeAndre are not together, but if we were, that's not something that I would have to tell you or anyone else."

Tamika rolled her eyes at Candice. As far as she was concerned, she was being secretive, and she didn't like it. Jenna just stood there looking at the exchange between the three. She already knew what was up with them, but she wasn't going to say anything to them about it. It wasn't her business, and frankly, she didn't care. She just wanted for everybody to be happy, she didn't care about the details. At that point, Tamika was stuck on if she wanted to remain friends with these girls or if she wanted to go her own way. They had been bumping heads lately, and she was losing the desire to make things right.

When the boat ride was over, DeAndre and Anthony linked up so they could go waterskiing. The girls didn't want to do that, so they stayed on the sidelines and cheered them on. That was the one thing that Anthony really wanted to do while they were there, and DeAndre really wanted to go snorkeling, and since the girls refused to do either of those activities, they figured they would do them together.

The group decided to go and eat lunch after the guys finished with their water activities. They looked like two little boys having the time of their lives. Jasmine was happy that Anthony was finally doing something fun and enjoyable. He was always so serious and so busy with his work that he didn't get much time to do anything fun, and she could tell that he really enjoyed himself.

Everybody was relieved to get a chance to sit down and

eat something. Breakfast was good, but it wore off a long time ago. They all talked amongst each other about the things they had done so far that day. They talked about the wedding and how beautiful everything was, and Jasmine thanked Anthony again about sending for her mother so that she could be there too. That meant so much to her, and she couldn't believe that he was able to keep that a secret. Even though the festivities of the day weren't over, Jasmine was the happiest that she'd been in a long time. She felt like if this was the beginning of the rest of her life that her life would be great. She was surrounded by people that genuinely cared for her, good experiences, and a little bit of excitement. It was all that she wanted. She was finally living drama free, and she loved every minute of it. She didn't feel like she was hard to please.

Tamika sat down at the far end of the table. Her body was there with the group, but her mind wasn't. She had been thinking about her relationship with her friends. She still loved them, but she felt like everything that had been going on was too much for her to handle. She had also been thinking about her boyfriend, who had been going through

238

a lot of stuff recently, and she couldn't even tell her friends about him. She had been hiding him from everybody for awhile now. She knew that they wouldn't understand their relationship, and she was already having issues with them, so she didn't want to make it worse. She wanted to be back at home to support him, and she wanted to be with her girls. She was stuck between the two.

Jasmine noticed that Tamika seemed to be in real deep thought and wanted to approach her, but she decided not to. She figured that if she sat that far away from her, then maybe she didn't want to be bothered, so she left her alone. She made a mental note to talk to her when the time was right. She wanted them to have the chance to air out everything and get all of their issues with one another on the table so that they could be fixed. She wanted her friend back. She didn't like the way their relationship had gone downhill, and she planned on making it right again.

"Jay, are you listening?" Anthony asked Jasmine. He had been talking to her, but she never responded. She was so wrapped up in her own thoughts that she didn't hear anything he or anyone else was saying.

Candice nudged Jasmine with her elbow. "Are you alright, girl?" Candice asked her when she finally got her attention.

"Yeah, I'm fine. Why?" Jasmine asked in an irritated tone.

"Anthony asked you a question."

"What's up?" she asked him.

"What do you want to do after this? After we eat," he said, noticing the confused look on her face.

"It doesn't matter. I'll do whatever you all decide."

"We were thinking about getting cleaned up and doing a little shopping," he told her.

"That's fine with me. We still have later today to do more of the water activities if you guys decide you want to do that again."

When they were done eating, they called the waitress over so that they could pay for their food. Anthony told them to go ahead and get themselves together and that he'd pay the bill. Everybody looked at him like he was crazy.

"Do you know how much all of this stuff cost?" somebody asked him.

"It doesn't matter. I got it."

"I ain't about to have no other man paying for my food. I'm a grown ass man," DeAndre said, standing up like that was going to make a difference. His comment made all of the women laugh.

"What the hell does being a grown ass man have to do with anything? This is my treat… my thank you to all of you for spending this special time with me and my wife. It's only food. I got it," Anthony told the group.

"Yeah, alright. Since you put it that way, I guess it's cool then. I appreciate it," DeAndre told him.

Anthony shook his head at DeAndre. He knew that he could pay for his own food, but he wanted to do something nice for everyone to show his appreciation for their support. He paid the bill and left a tip, and he and Jasmine headed to their suite. When she got there, she plopped down on the bed.

"Anthony you guys might have to go shopping without me."

"Why? What's up, Jay?"

"I don't feel well."

"You seemed fine a few minutes ago."

"I think it was something with the food I ate. It doesn't seem to be agreeing with me," she told him.

"Do you need to use the bathroom?" he asked her, thinking she just may have needed to do the number two.

"No. It's more than just my stomach. My head hurts, and I'm feeling dizzy."

"Damn, bae. I'm not going shopping and leaving you couped up in this room by yourself. I can stay with you and send everybody else on their way. We can go shopping another time. I'm more concerned about what's wrong with you."

"Please go," she begged. She didn't want him to spend the rest of his vacation trying to nurse her back to health.

"Jasmine, there's nothing to discuss here. If you are sick and staying here, then I'm going to stay here with you. That only makes sense. What are you talking about?"

"Fine, I'll go," Jasmine said, standing up to find her an outfit in her suitcase.

"You just said you don't feel well," Anthony told her, feeling confused as hell.

"And now, I'm saying I'll go shopping," she told him with an attitude.

She didn't want to talk about it anymore, so she grabbed her clothes and took them into the bathroom. She bent over to pick up something that she dropped, and when she stood up, she was extremely nauseated and feeling queasy. Her head was spinning, and she was dizzy, but she was determined to go out, even though she wasn't really feeling up to it because she didn't want to ruin anyone's trip.

Jasmine quickly showered, got dressed, and pulled her hair into a neat ponytail. When she walked out of the bathroom, Anthony was standing nearby with a box in his hand. She jumped because he startled her.

"What's that?" she asked him.

"It's a gift that I had for you last night. It's been sitting on the table this whole time. I'm surprised you hadn't seen it."

"I guess I overlooked it."

He handed it to her, and she put her bag down so that she could open it. She looked up at him and then at the box again. As soon as she opened it her mouth fell open. She couldn't believe how pretty it was.

"Anthony, this is beautiful. You didn't have to buy me this. You have done enough," she told him still in awe of the jewelry. It shined so much it was hard to look away from it.

"Shhh. Don't tell me what I can and can't buy for you. You are my woman. I'll do what I want for you."

His comment caught her off guard. She wasn't used to being spoken to that way. She had to catch herself from snapping at him because she didn't want to ruin the moment. She knew that he was just talking tough. He didn't mean anything by it.

He took the box from her and took the jewelry out of it. He sat the box down so that he could place the necklace around her neck. She looked in the mirror as he was connecting it in the back. She gasped at how pretty it was. It looked even better on than it did in the box. She stood in the mirror staring at it for a minute before turning to Anthony and thanking him for it.

"Hold on. That's not all," he said, taking the earrings

out of the box.

"I'll let you put these on yourself," he handed Jasmine the matching earrings. She took off the ones that she already had on and put the new ones in her ears. She checked herself out in the mirror from different angles so that she could see the jewelry sparkle under the light.

She walked over to Anthony and kissed him softly on his lips. "Thank you again, baby."

"Anything for you, Jay. You ready to go?"

"Let's go," she told him, leading the way out of the door.

Everybody else in the group were already outside waiting on them. Before she left out, she stopped by her mother's room so that she could check on her and Malcolm. They were singing and playing. She could tell that him being there was making her mother's day. Her mom looked like she was on cloud nine. After kissing her mother and her son, she and Ant left to join the rest of the group.

It was their last night on the beach, and they wanted to make the most of it. They had already done some of the water activities that they wanted to do. Now, they were about to see what the stores and shops were about. Jasmine didn't even expect it to be so many places to shop. Everywhere they went, she left with a bag or two. The guys didn't really get too many things. They just stayed behind the girls and let them run through the stores. The guys were the shopping bag holders.

"Girl, that necklace you got on is hot," Jenna told Jasmine while they waited for Candice to come out of the fitting room.

"Thank you. Anthony gave it to me today with these earrings to match," she replied, pointing to her ears.

"Aw man, those are really nice."

"What are y'all out here talking about?" Candice asked when she came out of the fitting room in a dress that showed every curve on her body. The dress was so nice that it caught DeAndre's attention all the way outside of the store. He, Anthony, and the other guys were standing by the store window waiting on the girls to come back out. It seemed like he turned around just in time to see Candice walking out of the fitting room. He couldn't keep his eyes off of her.

Anthony turned around to see what he was looking at. When he saw Candice standing in the little black dress, he laughed. He had to admit the dress was really becoming of her, but he knew DeAndre had it bad.

"Aye, man, what are you looking at?" Anthony teased, already knowing.

"Man, don't act like you don't see Candice over there in that lil' ass dress. I ain't never seen her wear nothing like that before," he told Anthony.

"That's because she's probably never worn anything like that before. Maybe she's feeling a little bit frisky today." Anthony laughed at his choice of words.

DeAndre didn't respond to Anthony. He knew that he was just messing with him. He didn't think she had it in her to wear something like that because he always saw her dressed so casually. If this was going to be a new thing for her, he was loving it already.

"Who are you wearing that for?" Tamika asked her.

"Hell, myself. Can't I want to look good for myself?"

"Yeah, yourself and DeAndre," Tamika replied,

continuing with her pettiness from earlier that day.

"You know what, girlfriend, I do like DeAndre. I'm starting to like him a lot, and word around town is he's kinda feeling me too, and if I want to look good for the man that I have feelings for, then that's what I'm going to do."

"Alright now," Jasmine said as she turned around and walked away. She heard all that she needed to hear. She had just witnessed Tamika get checked like homework. There was nothing more that needed to be said. Jasmine walked out of the store to mingle with the rest of her friends and family, and Jenna followed. Everybody left Tamika standing there looking dumb. It was nothing else she could say. She wanted to know what was going on with Candice and DeAndre, and she found out.

"Hey, baby, what's going on?" Anthony greeted Jasmine when she got outside. He noticed the expression that she had on her face and asked her what was going on. He could tell that the mood between the girls had changed.

"Oh nothing. Just girl drama," she told him.

"How are you feeling?" he asked her.

"A lot better. I don't know what was up with me earlier," she lied. She wasn't feeling that much better. She kept drinking a lot of water to keep herself from overheating and feeling nauseated, but she was still feeling dizzy and light headed.

"That's good. I'm glad you are doing better. You had me worried about you. How you get sick on our wedding weekend?" He stood behind her and wrapped his arms around her waist.

Candice came walking out of the store with her bag in her hand. She bought the dress that she tried on and a few other things as well. They did a little more shopping before calling it quits. They wanted to have a group dinner since it was their last night there, and the sun was already starting to go down. Everybody took all of their shopping bags to their rooms and met up on the beach so they could head to dinner. Jasmine invited her mom, but she declined the offer.

When they came back out, Candice was dressed in the dress that she purchased while at the store. She had on coordinating sandals and jewelry. The dress was all black and stopped mid-thigh. It was solid from the top to her waist line, exposing her cleavage, and the rest was sheer with a lace design embroidered on it.

"Girl, you look like you trying to catch you a man tonight," Jenna teased her.

"Well, I know that I don't have to look too far."

DeAndre noticed a few of the guys that were at the wedding looking at Candice, and it wasn't the first time. He saw them checking her out a few times. He didn't say anything, although he didn't like it, because she wasn't his girl officially. He knew that she was able to choose anybody she wanted, but that didn't stop him from keeping a lookout. He wasn't going to let anyone else push up on her after he already got her warmed up.

He mean mugged one of the guys as he walked passed him, never breaking eye contact. He walked up on Candice and asked her where her clothes were. He didn't say it loud enough for anyone else to hear him. Candice laughed and told him that she had her clothes on. He did not approve. He told her that when she tried the dress on earlier that day that he thought it was something that was supposed to be worn in the bedroom not out in public.

"What is the problem here, Dre?" she asked slightly flattered but also annoyed.

"The problem is that you are out here in lingerie, and you got random men looking at you."

"Boy, this is not lingerie, it's a dress. You are trippin'," she told him, laughing. "And I don't care about what men are looking at me. I didn't wear it for them."

"Well, who did you wear it for?"

"You like?" she asked as she twirled around in a circle.

"You wore this dress for me?" he asked with a huge smile on his face. He didn't want to show his excitement, but he couldn't hold back his smile.

"I had you in mind when I bought it. I thought that you would like it."

"I love it, C. You are beautiful in anything that you wear though."

"I appreciate that. I just wanted to do something a little bit different tonight."

"Well, I'm glad you did it."

Anthony came back from making arrangements for

them to have dinner on the beach. He was told that it would take a little while to set up since he didn't plan for it sooner. He and Jasmine walked along the beach while they waited. They talked about how excited they were to be spending the rest of their of their lives together and how they hated that it took so long for them to get to the point that they were at.

Tamika decided that she didn't want to be a part of the group for dinner. Instead, she stayed back in her room and ate dinner there. She wanted to check up on her boyfriend to see how he was doing. She hadn't talked to him much since she had been gone. She missed his company, and the more she saw Anthony and Jasmine together, the more she was reminded of how much she missed him.

Jenna stayed at the meetup spot and enjoyed the view. She was content right there. The atmosphere was calm and peaceful, and she enjoyed everything about being there. She knew that she was going to miss the beach when she got back to St. Louis.

Anthony's cell phone rang. It was someone from the resort informing him that their tables were set up for dinner. They had a tent with lights in it that just made the ambiance radiant and welcoming. The tables were dressed beautifully, and they had lit candles as the centerpieces. Once everyone was seated, the waiter took drink orders. Jasmine felt like she was starving to death. She wanted to order something to eat right then and there, but she figured she'd go in the order that the meal was supposed to go. When she ordered her drink, she also ordered a glass of water. She felt like she needed the water to help the alcohol go down.

When the drinks arrived, everybody put in the orders for their appetizers and entrées. After the waiter walked away, Anthony stood up and made a toast, thanking everyone for coming and spending the weekend with them once again. DeAndre also made a toast to the newly married couple. He expressed his love for them and wished them the best. He told Anthony that he better treat her right because she was a good girl. He didn't care what anyone thought about it. No matter who he fell for, he would always have a soft spot in his heart for Jasmine. He had seen her through so many tough times and nurtured her through too many things not to.

The night went great, the food was delicious, and everyone genuinely enjoyed each other's company. Nobody even really missed Tamika. It was kind of a relief that she wasn't there to bring down the mood at dinner. They didn't have a band or anything special, but one of the guests played some music on their cell phone, and everyone danced and partied. They kept the drinks flowing as long as people were drinking them.

Jasmine and Anthony excused themselves first. They were done for the night. They went back to their room for an instant replay of the activities from the night before, but everybody stayed a little bit longer. DeAndre noticed the same guy from earlier still staring at Candice, and as bad as he wanted to say something to the guy, he didn't. Instead, he got up and danced with her. She was already up, dancing by herself, minding her own business. She didn't even realize that she was being watched. Jenna sat back and watched what was going on between DeAndre and the other guy. She thought that it was funny how DeAndre was trying to claim Candice, and Candice had no clue about the silent beef that DeAndre had with the guy. When he and DeAndre made eye contact, the other guy just walked away. DeAndre hoped that would be the last that he ever saw of him.

"Come on, C. You ready to go?" he asked her.

"Where are we going? I'm having a good time right here."

"I don't know. Let's go for a walk."

"We can't just leave Jenna here."

"Jenna, me and Candice want to go for a walk. You cool here by yourself?" he asked her.

"I'm good, y'all. Go have fun," Jenna told them.

Candice grabbed her purse and told Jenna that she'd meet her in their room later. She held DeAndre's hand as they strolled along the beach. The night air was cool and relaxing. Candice stopped to take off her shoes so that she could feel the sand between her toes as the water rushed against her legs.

"This has been a beautiful trip, don't you think?" DeAndre asked her as they stopped to watch the waves. He stood behind her and held her around her waist.

She turned around to face him. She didn't say anything right away. She just looked at him and took in all of his features. She didn't know why she never realized how fine he was. His honey complexion was everything. His eyes were dark brown, and his facial features were big just like she liked. His hair was low cut and had waves for days.

"Kiss me, DeAndre."

"What? Where did that come from?" he questioned.

"I want you to kiss me. This time, you have my permission."

"As bad as I want to kiss you, I know that you have had a lot to drink. I don't want to do something that you are going to regret tomorrow."

Candice placed each of her hands on his face and kissed his lips. She continued to kiss him until he gave in and kissed her back. He had no idea if she really wanted this or if it was the alcohol talking. They all had a lot to drink at dinner. She slid her hands underneath his shirt and rubbed his chest intensely. She raised his shirt over his head and let it fall to the ground. Candice unbuckled his belt and slid her hand down the front of his shorts and started to fondle his manhood.

DeAndre backed up to break himself out of her grasp. "C, what are you doing? Chill out, girl."

"Dre, come on. I want you, and I want you now," she said in a whiny voice.

"Girl, you are tipsy, and we are outside."

"We are the only people right here, and I know what I want, tipsy or not. So, are you going to give it to me, or not?" she challenged.

Going against his better judgment, he gave her what she said she wanted. DeAndre made love to Candice on the beach in the Bahamas. When they were done, he felt a little unsure of their situation. The sex was good, but he just hoped that whatever it was they had lasted far beyond the beach. He wanted it to continue even after they returned home. They didn't really do too much talking. He walked Candice to her room that she shared with Jenna and returned back to his room.

CHAPTER NINETEEN

Sleep didn't come easy for Candice the night before. She was wide awake and full of smiles just thinking about what she had done. Even though Jenna inquired several times, she wouldn't tell her that she and DeAndre got down when they left her at dinner. She wanted to keep her little secret to herself for a little while… at least until after she talked to him again. She didn't fall asleep until well after three in the morning and was back up again at six. She had to pack her bags and meet up with Tamika, Jasmine, Jenna, Anthony, and DeAndre to catch their flight back home. Regardless of how tired she was, she was still on cloud nine.

Jasmine had gotten up early to make sure that she had everything packed for her, Anthony, and Malcolm. Her mom had kept Malcolm overnight so that she and Anthony could enjoy their last night in the Bahamas alone. She never imagined her wedding, reception, or the days that followed to be so amazing. She watched Anthony while he slept. She couldn't believe that she had actually been blessed to finally be with the man that she should have been with in the first place. Although she knew that without Corey she wouldn't have her son and for him, she'd do it all over again. She made sure that she had everything together with the clothes that they were to wear to the airport laid out for them.

Tamika was the first one up and out. She left her room before checkout time. She had her bag packed and was already at the airport waiting. She was so ready to go. She enjoyed the wedding and the reception, but everything else after that was just a waste of her time, and she wanted nothing more than to be back in St. Louis in the arms of her boyfriend.

Jasmine called around to make sure everybody was up and getting themselves together. She wanted them to have time to eat before they left. That's when she found out that Tamika was already at the airport waiting for them. She couldn't believe that Tamika had left them, but she was so sick of her she didn't even trip off of it. She figured that she could sit there and wait or try to catch an earlier flight. She didn't care anymore.

259

"Jas, I'm getting up now. I need to take a quick shower and throw my stuff in my bag," DeAndre told her, yawning into the phone. He rolled out of the bed super tired but excited to finally see Candice again, although he was a little nervous. He knew that their session on the beach was good to him, but he didn't know how she felt about it. He couldn't believe that he was really smitten by her after them being friends for so long, but it was something that he couldn't control and didn't want to.

"Hey, Jas, Candice is packed up and in the shower already, and I'm packing now. We'll be ready by the time you guys are ready to head to breakfast," Jenna told her when she called. Jasmine was happy that everybody was on schedule. Now, all that was left for her to do was to wake Anthony up. She wanted to let him sleep in a little longer because he was always up and doing so much. She knew that when they got back home it would be the same way.

Once he was up, she called her mother to make sure that she was up and getting Malcolm ready. She told her what time she needed them to meet for breakfast. This time, her mom agreed to go. She knew that once she got back home, there was no telling how long it would be before she was able to see her daughter and grandson again. Jasmine didn't get to visit that often, and she wasn't supposed to travel. She wanted to spend the last few hours with them as a group because she didn't know if it would be her last.

About a half hour later, everybody met at the agreed location. Jasmine and Anthony were so excited to reunite with Malcolm. It seemed as if they hadn't seen him in so long. They hugged and kissed him over and over again. Jasmine hugged her mom and thanked her for keeping Malcolm so that she and Anthony could spend some time alone.

All of the women got on the shuttle that was taking them to the restaurant while the guys loaded the luggage. Everybody was so tired. They didn't talk much. They all seemed to be wrapped up in their own thoughts. The ride to the restaurant wasn't long enough. Anthony tried to catch a quick nap on the way but couldn't.

When they were finally able to be seated DeAndre

pulled a chair out for Candice to sit down. She sat down and motioned for him to sit right next to her. His approach was so unexpected, but everybody noticed it. He assumed that everybody already knew that they had a thing for each other, so he didn't see the need to hide it.

"How you feel?" he leaned over and whispered to her.

"I'm okay… tired. How are you?" she asked.

"I feel good. I didn't get much sleep, but it was well worth it," he replied with a huge smile on his face.

"What was well worth it?" she asked him as if she didn't already know what he was talking about.

"You're going to make me say it in front of all these people?"

"I just want to know what was well worth you not getting enough sleep."

"Dancing with you at dinner, and making love to you on the beach last night was well worth me not getting enough sleep last night," he told her licking his lips.

Just to hear him say the words made her panties wet. "So you're saying that you love me?" she asked him, hoping that he'd say no.

That question caught him off guard. He didn't want to say the wrong thing, but he had to be real with her. "I can't say that I love you as my woman C, but I've loved you as my friend for a long time. I hope that what happened last night didn't mess up our friendship. I hope when we get back home we can keep this going—"

"The sex?" she asked, cutting him off.

"That would be nice too, but even if we didn't do it again, I want to try this relationship thing with you. Is that what you want? I wasn't even trying to have sex with you last night because I knew that you had too much to drink, and I didn't want you to regret it the next day."

"DeAndre, chill, boo. It's good. I don't regret anything that happened. I told you last night what I wanted, and I got it. Stop tripping."

"Y'all over there having a whole conversation. Can we know what y'all are talking about?" Anthony asked, being nosy.

Candice was getting ready to respond, but the waitress came to take their orders before she could. *Thank God,* she thought to herself. She knew she wasn't about to tell them the truth, and DeAndre didn't look like he was about to tell them anything. The man had her feeling like a schoolgirl with a crush. The whole relationship bloomed out of nowhere. Ever since the night Malcolm was taken, she and DeAndre had been inseparable. She wanted the same thing he did. She was hoping that this relationship was something that could prosper and not something that just came about because of her vulnerability.

The group had a good time at breakfast. After all the food they had and a few cups of coffee, they were wide awake. It seems like once the food came, they forgot all about interrogating Candice and DeAndre. Jasmine's mom fell in love with all of Jasmine's friends. She knew that her daughter had a good support system around her, and once she went back home, she wouldn't have to worry about her anymore.

When they were done eating, they returned to their shuttle and headed to the airport. As much as they loved their trip, they all were anxious to get back home. The guys had business to take care of, Candice and Jenna had to get back to work, and Jasmine was ready to get back to her regular schedule with Malcolm. Jasmine's mom cried when they walked her to her gate. Her crying made everybody else cry. Of course, the guys tried to hold back the tears, but the girls cried like babies. She didn't want to let her daughter and grandson go. She hugged and kissed Anthony and thanked him over and over for sending for her so that she could see her daughter get married. She hugged and kissed all of Jasmine's friends and wished them the best. At her request, they all held hands and she said a prayer over all of them. She said a general prayer for everybody, and she put a few specifics in there for each of them. That alone made them all cry even more.

They hugged one last time and watched as she boarded her plane before making their way to their plane. When they arrived at their gate, they saw Tamika sitting there. She had been there for hours. Nobody really wanted to say anything to her because they didn't like the way she had been acting, but Anthony forced himself to speak.

"Hey, Tamika... we missed you at breakfast. You been here the whole time?" he asked her.

"Yep, I've been here waiting for you guys. I didn't

265

want to eat." She kept it short.

"Well, we here now," he said, being a smart ass.

"This is going to be a long ass trip back home. We still have to get on a connecting flight just like when we came," Jenna said.

As soon as they sat down to rest, their gate was being called to board.

Jasmine, Anthony, and Tamika sat in a row together. Jenna and Candice were supposed to sit together and DeAndre's seat was somewhere else. Before they sat down, Jenna had already decided to give her seat up to DeAndre so that he and Candice could sit together, and she sat in his seat. As soon as the wheels were up and they headed home, Anthony laid his head on Jasmine's shoulder and got comfortable for the flight. Tamika put her earbuds in to tune everybody out. Jenna pulled out a book that she was reading, and DeAndre and Candice sat there and talked the entire time.

The flight was short, but after they switched flights, they all resumed what they were doing on the first one. Jasmine adjusted herself between Anthony on her shoulder and Malcolm sitting on her lap squirming. Emotionally and mentally, she was in such a good place. She had just had the best time of her life. She couldn't have asked for a better time. She felt truly blessed.

When the flight landed at Lambert International Airport in St. Louis, Jasmine kissed the top of Anthony's head and whispered in his ear, "Baby, we're home. It's time to get up." The first kiss didn't work, so she tried it again. The second time was a charm. He lifted his head up and kissed her back. When they were finally allowed to get up, Tamika was the first one up. She grabbed her bag from the overhead compartment and waited for her chance to leave.

Once the other passengers were out of her way, she walked off the plane, and the rest of the group followed behind her. They went and got their luggage from the luggage claim and then went outside to where Anthony had cars waiting for them to take each of them to their own homes. Not everyone's car was there yet, so as they waited for their cars to arrive, they all stood outside telling jokes and playing around with each other. Tamika made a phone call to her boyfriend to tell him that they were back and that she was going to get dropped off at his house when her ride arrived.

A few minutes after hanging up her phone, a man ran up on Candice toting a Mini Draco AK47. Nobody saw him coming, but everybody knew who he was when they laid eyes on him. Immediately, Anthony jumped in front of her to try to stop the gunman from shooting, but it was no point. He pulled the trigger and sent bullets through Anthony and Candice. The other airport patrons screamed and ran for cover. Everything happened so fast that the others didn't have time to react.

Jasmine saw Anthony and Candice hit the ground, and she froze. She couldn't move. Her worst nightmare was taking place right in front of her eyes, and she wasn't even sleeping. It was obvious that Kerry knew his target when he got there because he didn't even go after anybody else. DeAndre attempted to charge at Kerry, but Kerry had put the gun to his head and shot himself, which made DeAndre stop in his tracks. When Kerry pulled the trigger on himself Jasmine, Jenna, and DeAndre heard Tamika yell out to

Kerry, and she ran to his side.

"Kerry, baby, what did you do?" she asked, shaking him, knowing that he wasn't going to get up.

"What the fuck do you mean 'Kerry, baby?'" DeAndre yelled, standing over Tamika.

DeAndre looked over at Candice and Anthony laying on the ground in pools of their own blood. He knew that there was no more life in them. He walked over to Candice and dropped to his knees. He leaned over her and whispered to her as his tears covered her face. He hoped for the best and checked for a pulse, and there wasn't one. He moved over to where his brother was. He checked for a pulse on Anthony, and he was already gone too. Covered in Anthony and Candice's blood, DeAndre walked over to Jasmine, wrapped his arms around her, and squeezed her as tight as he could.

Jenna walked over to them and took Malcolm. She was speechless. There was nothing she could say to make this right or to make it make sense. Tamika stood up and looked at Jasmine with sympathy in her eyes. She knew how this all looked, but she didn't have anything to do with what

Kerry did. She had been talking to him on and off while she was out of town, and he never mentioned anything about wanting to hurt anyone. She would never have let her friends walk into that situation without warning. She would have tried to talk him out of it or something.

"Jasmine, I am so sorry—"

"Tamika, if you don't get away from me, you'll be next," Jasmine told her through gritted teeth before she could finish her apology.

Jasmine walked over to her husband lying on the ground surrounded by strangers. She could hear the paramedics coming. She heard police sirens. She heard people mumbling about what they thought they knew about what happened and why. She laid down next to him and cried uncontrollably. There was no point in trying to console her. It couldn't be done. She had been on cloud nine the whole time she'd been gone, and now, her heart was shattered into a million pieces.

Jenna wanted to break down just looking at the violent scene in front of her, but she had to be strong for them. She had to be there for her friends the best way she could. One was gone, and two were grieving. Tamika knew it wasn't her fault, but she was definitely guilty by association. She didn't know how she was going to get them to believe that it wasn't her, but she wanted to be there to console them, and she couldn't even do that.

The paramedics had to come and pry Jasmine away from Anthony. When they did, she just moved over to Candice.

"Why would you leave me like this, Candice? You *and* Anthony! You *and* Anthony!" she began to yell at her friend.

Another paramedic pulled her away from Candice and sat her on the ground nearby. She got up made her way over to Tamika. "You, bitch! You set us up. You knew this whole time that Kerry was going to be here! You knew this whole time that he was coming for Candice, and you didn't say anything."

"I didn't know—"

Before Tamika could finish her statement, Jasmine stood up and kicked her in the face, causing Tamika to fall backward. Jasmine stomped her continuously until

DeAndre pulled her off of her. DeAndre, Jasmine, and Jenna stayed with Candice and Anthony until they were taken away. Even after that, it was hard for them to leave. They were paralyzed from the pain they felt.

Jenna made sure that they got back to Jasmine's house. She stayed with them so that she could help with Malcolm. She knew that Jasmine couldn't do it alone. She and DeAndre stayed couped up in her house for days before they could bring themselves to do anything or to go anywhere. Jenna tried to talk to each of them separately, but neither of them would talk. They both shut down completely.

DeAndre was pissed that Kerry killed himself like a coward. He felt like he took that satisfaction away from him. He would have loved to be the one to kill him. He would have easily killed for Candice and Anthony. There were no words to express the hurt he felt. His brother and his friend were gone.

"They were just here. We were just together," DeAndre would say over and over again. He couldn't wrap his mind around how fast they were taken away from him. He wanted to be strong for Jasmine, but he couldn't be strong for himself. The blow took the wind out of him. Every time he heard her cry, his heart broke a little bit more. He knew that his loss was great, but her loss was greater. On the fifth day of moping around, he finally got up and left. He went back to his apartment. He couldn't stand to hear Jasmine cry every day and know that he couldn't do anything to fix what was wrong.

Jenna had to take a few extra days off from work because she didn't feel comfortable leaving Jasmine alone with the baby. Her thinking was a little twisted, and she didn't want her to do anything to harm him. She cooked meals, but Jasmine wouldn't eat them. She ran baths for her, but she wouldn't get in them. She even tried to comb her hair for her, but Jasmine just refused. Jasmine went back and forth from blaming God for her best friend and husbands murder, to blaming Corey, then blaming Candice. She thought that if only Candice would not have killed Corey, none of it would have happened. Then, she thought that if Corey wasn't such a nut case, nobody would have felt the need to murder him. Her mind was going in circles trying to figure out why all of it had happened.

When DeAndre got back to his apartment, he broke down in the middle of his living room floor. He cried for himself, he cried for Jasmine, and he cried for Malcolm. It hit him hard. He'd never cared for anyone like he cared for his friends. Sometimes in life, that's all you had, and that's all he had. He knew he had to pull it together sooner than later because he knew that he had to be strong for Jasmine and Malcolm, but right then, he needed his time to grieve alone. He was angry, and he wanted to do something to somebody. The person he wanted to get at was already dead. The only outlet he could think of was going to the gym, so he did just that. After a quick shower, he headed to the gym to push some weights around in hopes to feel a little better. He knew that it wouldn't help him emotionally, but it could at least allow him to let off some steam.

He was in such deep thought that he didn't even realize the girl that was watching him from across the room. She had been watching him for a while, but he was in his zone. She approached him. "Hey, can you spot me over there?"

she asked, pointing to the bench press bar.

Before saying anything he looked her over and realized how pretty she was. She was had a milk chocolate complexion, long straight hair, a beauty mark that sat perfectly above her top lip, and her body was banging. He didn't even try to mask the fact that he was checking her out. He boldly looked over every curve of her body which wasn't hard to do with the black leggings, and her purple sports bra she had on. She wasn't trying to hide anything and he wasn't trying to hide the fact that he was looking.

"So, are you going to help me?" She asked growing tired of him gawking at her like he hadn't seen a woman in years.

"Naw, I'm going to have to pass," he told her, continuing to lift the weights that he had in his hands.

"Seriously?" she asked him not believing that after all of the staring he had done he had the nerve to turn her down.

"Yes, seriously," he firmly stated.

The girl was embarrassed that she had just been turned down. She wasn't used to that at all. Any other day

DeAndre would have helped her but on this day, he just wasn't feeling it. He couldn't deny that the girl was fine but his head was not in the right place to be entertaining someone else. He didn't even want to talk to anyone. He just wanted to stay in his zone where he coldn't be bothered and that's just what he did. From that day forward DeAndre just focused on getting money, and tying up some loose ends that Anthoy left behind. He didn't make time for women; he couldn't focus on their needs like they expected him to, so he didn't even try. Besides, he was still grieving the loss of Candice. Before she passed, he had known for sure that they were going to be together, and he was so excited about the thought of it all, and then before it could happen, tragedy struck, and he had no control over it. He couldn't change the outcome, he couldn't fix it, and he was still dealing with that. He knew that in time, he would be okay, but until then, he was riding solo, and all he cared about was making sure Jasmine and her kids didn't want for anything.

The End

Epilogue

Tamika kept her distance. She reached out to Jasmine and Jenna a few times, but she was unsuccessful in getting anywhere with Jasmine. Jasmine didn't want to have anything to do with her. She felt like Tamika set them up, and she thought that Tamika knew that Kerry planned on murdering them or at least Candice because she murdered his brother. Jasmine felt like Tamika was real shady because she never told anyone that she was dating Kerry. She was sleeping with the enemy the whole time, but truth was, Kerry approached her shortly after he'd seen her at the hospital when she was there visiting Jasmine after she got shot. He had seen her out and about and pushed up on her. She knew who he was because looked just like Corey and she rejected him several times, but his persistence paid off eventually. She did tell him about where Corey was after they left his body in the warehouse. That's how he knew where to find him. She told him about Anthony, DeAndre, and Jasmine being at the warehouse, and that's how he was able to steal Anthony's car. After she left Jasmine's house the night that she and Anthony brought

Malcolm back home, she went to Kerry's house and told him that Corey had been shot. She told him that Candice pulled the trigger, but it was an accident. Tamika wasn't snitching on her friends intentionallu. She thought that she was just conversing with her man. She didn't want to keep any secrets from him but she didn't know that he was building a case against them the whole time. She was definitely his inside man, and she didn't even realize it. She let her jealousy and personal feelings for Jasmine get in the way of her better judgment.

Tamika knew that if she ever got a chance to explain it all to Jasmine that she wouldn't care and that it would be pointless, so she didn't even try anymore. She accepted the fact that their friendship was over, and she felt the safest thing for her to do was to stay away. Shortly after the incident, she broke her lease and moved back to Oklahoma with some of her relatives so that she could get away from the drama and they could help her get back on her feet.

Jasmine, DeAndre, and Jenna were able to pull themselves together long enough to plan a double funeral for Anthony and Candice. They decided to do it together because neither of them felt like they had the strength to do it more than once. They made sure that they both were laid to rest beautifully. Both of their caskets had details that resembled them as they were on earth. The ceremony was short and sweet. Friends and family from each family came out to celebrate their lives instead of their deaths. They recited poems, sang songs, and Jasmine stood up and read a letter that she wrote to each of them. The burial was the hardest part for Jasmine. To watch them lowered into the ground made everything real. Thankfully, DeAndre was there to hold her up. They had a repass, but Jasmine didn't stay the entire time. She went back home to grieve in peace.

One month after the funeral, Jasmine sat in the driveway of her house that she shared with Anthony and her son. It was the house that Anthony begged her to move into in order to keep her safe and away from harm. It was the same house that he encouraged her to put her finishing touches on to make it their home. She hadn't been in the house very long, but she had grown to love it. Every room in the house had a piece of her in it, but every room in the house had a piece of Anthony in it too, and that she couldn't take. She couldn't live in the house anymore knowing that his spirit was all through there. She couldn't wake up every day in the same bedroom that they shared knowing that he would never be there to lay on his side of the bed again. Some parts of the house even smelled like him. There was no way she could stay there. She couldn't handle it.

Jasmine looked over the outside of the house. She looked at the flowers that she had grown and she thought of the day she moved in. She thought about the times that she and her friends hung out there. She put her truck in drive and drove around the crescent-shaped driveway with Malcolm asleep in the back seat. After so many tears and so many meltdowns, she had finally gotten to the point of being able to pull herself together enough to pack her and Malcolm's things. She decided not to take everything. She just took with her the things that she definitely needed and the things that held some kind of sentimental value. She made sure to take some of Anthony's personal belongings too. They had so much stuff, but it wasn't hard for her to choose what was most important to her. She packed up her truck with everything that would fit, and DeAndre agreed to drive a UHaul to her new home and deliver the rest of her items. She wanted to get a head start and get on the road, so she left him to close everything up at the house. She knew that he and Anthony had gotten really close and often referred to each other as brothers. She didn't know what Anthony had that DeAndre would want to remember him by, but she allowed DeAndre to take a few things that once belonged to Anthony so that he could have something of him. The house was in her name, so it was hers. She couldn't decide if she wanted to sell it or not, so she just locked it up tight and left. She decided that she'd figure all of that out at a later time.

On the highway, she couldn't help but cry at the thought of losing her husband. Hell, they had only been married for a few days before he was permanently taken away from her. Now, her son didn't have a father, and she didn't have a companion. It seemed like as soon as things started looking up for her, a dark cloud came along and hovered over her. There was no reason that he shouldn't be there with them. Not to mention, she lost a friend too. She knew that Tamika had changed a little bit, but she didn't think that she would stoop to the low levels of evil and deceit that she did. Someone that was supposed to be her best friend set her and her man up and had been doing it for months right in front of their faces.

As far as she was concerned, there was no love in St. Louis. She tried to have love and have meaningful relationships, but it failed her every time. There were no perfect love stories. There were no happily ever afters... nothing. She developed a hate for the city that raised her and everybody in it. She found an apartment in Atlanta for her and her son to stay until she could get on her feet and probably find a house. She had no idea what her new city would have to offer her she just remembered traveling there before, and she knew that she loved it so much that she didn't want to leave. It was something about the wind. It blew differently than in St. Louis. The people were different in many ways, and it seemed like the sun shined brighter there. She didn't know if it would be her permanent spot, but she had to leave St. Louis anyway, so she figured she'd give it a try.

DeAndre made it to Jasmine's new apartment a few hours after her. He made sure that he set up her and Malcolm's beds when he first got there. He unloaded his UHaul, but he didn't set anything else up. They went out to dinner that night, and when they got back to the apartment, he made a pallet on the floor in the living room while Jasmine slept in her room, and Malcolm slept in his. It was hard for him to sleep with Jasmine crying in the next room. The walls in her apartment were paper thin, and he was able to hear every sniff and every whimper. It broke his heart to see her in so much pain. It was so much different than him trying to comfort her after Corey beat her ass. She was hurt over the loss of her husband and best friend—the man that she planned on spending the rest of her life with. He didn't know if he should let her cry alone in her room or if he should make the attempt to comfort her. He promised her a long time ago that whatever happened in her life, he would always be there for her. He too was hurting. The one person that he rocked with when everything started going downhill with Corey was

Anthony. It was almost as if he picked up where Corey left off. As soon as he and Candice started getting close, she was tragically taken away. DeAndre didn't have many friends. It wasn't an easy task to make friends. You couldn't trust people enough to let them get close to you. He cherished his friendships because he knew they didn't come around too often.

DeAndre knew that Anthony would want him to take care of Jasmine and Malcolm to the best of his ability. He even put him up on some of his business deals so that he could keep some money in his pocket. He never knew the kind of feelings that DeAndre had for Jasmine before he came along. Besides, they were friends first anyway. When DeAndre noticed her getting serious about Anthony, he put his feelings for her on the back burner, and when he started developing feelings for Candice, he cut all of his feelings for Jasmine off.

Jasmine stayed to herself a lot once she had gotten settled in her new place. There were a few neighbors that came around from time to time, wanting to have small talk whenever they saw her sitting outside on her porch or coming and going. She engaged in a little conversation, but she never gave up any personal information. She knew that they were just being nosy anyway. They always wanted to know where she was from, how old she was, did she work, and why she relocated to Atlanta. One guy came to her one day while she was getting groceries out of her truck, and instead of offering to help her with her bags, he told her, "I see your license plates say you're from Missouri. What part of are you from? Tell me you're from St. Louis. Tell me you know Nelly. You know, 'it's goin down down, baby. Uh ohhhhhh.'" She couldn't believe it. She lied. She told him that she wasn't from St. Louis, but she was from Blue Springs, Missouri. He looked a little disappointed, but she didn't care. She didn't want to be bothered.

DeAndre stayed in Atlanta with Jasmine and Malcolm for a few weeks to help her get settled and to get a feel of the neighborhood and her surroundings. He didn't want to leave them in an unfamiliar place with people they didn't know. He wanted to make sure everything was good before he left. Jasmine started getting into a routine with Malcolm, and she even enrolled herself into nursing school. DeAndre stayed with the baby while she did that and gave her time to put him in daycare. When she had all of her business taken care of and was okay being on her own, he decided it was time for him to leave and take care of some business of his own. He didn't want to spend too much time there while both of them were still vulnerable. There were a few times he began thinking that with Candice and Anthony out of the way he might finally have his chance with Jasmine, but with him and Anthony being friends, the dynamic of that changed, and he knew that was never going to be a possibility.

Before he left, Jasmine sat him down to tell him something that she had been holding in since right after the funeral. She revealed to him that she was pregnant with Anthony's baby. She found out shortly after Anthony was murdered, and she didn't even get a chance to tell him before he passed that he was going to have his own biological child. DeAndre was the first person to know. She asked DeAndre if he could be the godfather to that child, and of course, he agreed. He hugged her tightly, kissed her cheek, handed her a few stacks, and caught a flight back to St. Louis. When he left, he was more confused with the news he had just gotten than he was before. They spoke on the phone several times a day, and he made sure to not let too much time go by without visiting her. He felt like it was his duty to see after her and Malcolm. DeAndre knew that she had money from the accounts that Anthony had in her name, but whenever he came to visit, he always gave her a few stacks to put up for a rainy day. When the baby was due, he made sure he was there. He welcomed Anthony's daughter into the world and cut her umbilical cord. It was a bittersweet moment for the both of them, but he kept his promise to always be there for her no matter what.

Jasmine made sure to keep in touch with Jenna. In fact, she had plans on going to Atlanta to visit soon. She was excited to see her friend and to meet the new member to the family. Although they were in two different states, they made sure to keep their friendship strong. They were all they had, and they made sure to embrace their friendship and let it flourish even with many miles between them.

Be sure to LIKE our Major Key

Publishing page on Facebook!